DANGER ON SEVENTH STREET

Book Two

JERRY D. THOMAS

Pacific Press® Publishing Association
Nampa, Idaho
Oshawa, Ontario, Canada

Editor: Aileen Andres Sox
Designer: Robert N. Mason
Illustration/Art Direction: Justinen Creative Group
Typeset in Century Old Style 13/17

ISBN 0-8163-1658-9

Dedication

To all the little people who inspired these stories:

First, to my own wonderful children—Jonathan, Jennifer, and Jeremy—who aren't so little anymore. Not all the stories are about them—just the good ones.

And then to my brothers and sisters—in memory of the days when we were kids and of the escapades we shared. Also, to my nieces and nephews on both sides of the family—thanks for the stories you inspired.

Finally, to all the kids who will read these stories or hear them read. May the stories bring you smiles, laughter, help in difficult situations, hope for a bright tomorrow, and a belief in the never-ending love of God.

A few words of thanks:

To the management of Pacific Press for having the vision to publish this set.

To Aileen Andres Sox, who encouraged me from the beginning.

To Robert Mason for a design that will drag kids right into the pages.

To Lars and Kim Justinen and their creative group for the outstanding art that brings the stories to life.

And most of all, to my wife, Kitty, for her love and patient endurance while these stories were being written.

Contents

Escape From Zoomania

Zap, zap. Run, jump. Faster, faster, faster!

Doug stared at the TV screen and pressed the buttons of his video game. "Take that! Gotcha!" he murmured to the characters on the screen.

"Doug, did you eat your breakfast?"

Doug's eyes never budged from the screen. His fingers moved faster than ever.

"Douglas!" Mom stood in front of the TV. "Turn that thing off and come eat."

"Just a minute, Mom," Doug whined. When she didn't move, he pushed the Pause button. "Oh, all right."

Dad looked up from behind his paper. "I'm so glad you could join us, son. Have some pancakes."

Doug sat. "Dad, you should see how I got by the rolling hedgehogs—I had to climb all the way over the giraffe wall."

Dad lifted one eyebrow. "Rolling hedgehogs?"

"It's my Escape From Zoomania game," Doug explained.

Playing video, computer games

"You know, you're trapped in the center of a zoo where all the animals got loose? And you have to find your way out past all the animals? And all you have to protect yourself is a stun gun?"

"Oh," Dad said as he nodded, "that game. Well, good luck." He went back to his paper.

"Doug, what are you planning to do today?" Mom asked. "Not just sit in front of that game, I hope."

"Oh, Mom. I've got lots of things to do today. I just want to beat this game first." Doug attacked his pancakes with his fork.

Mom looked at him over her glass of milk. "It seems like you've been playing that game every day this week. When was the last time you played outside? When was the last time you played with Nathan?"

Doug rolled his eyes. "Mom, I've been outside every day walking home from school. And just this week I invited Nathan over to play."

Nathan said he didn't want to play Zoomania, so he didn't come over, Doug said to himself. *But I invited him, so it's not my fault.*

"I'm glad your like you video game, Doug," Mom said. "But there are still other fun things to do. And this will be a good day to do something else. Something outside. Like your father will be doing. You were mowing the lawn today, weren't you, dear?"

Dad peeked over the top of the paper. "I'm not sure. The paper says there's a good chance of rain this afternoon. Maybe even thunderstorms."

"Then maybe you should mow this morning and read the paper this afternoon," Mom suggested.

Doug decided that now was a good time to put his plate in the sink and disappear. In just a few seconds, he was back dodging elephants and outrunning bighorn sheep.

After an hour or so, Dad stopped by on his way to the door. "Hey, Doug, want to run down to the hardware store with me? The lawn mower won't start, and I have to pick up a few things to fix it."

Normally, Doug loved going to the hardware store with his dad. They always spent time looking around, buying things they didn't need that day—but were sure to need soon.

This time, Doug waved his dad off. "No, thanks," he said, his fingers flying over the buttons.

Dad frowned. "Doug, I'm sure that's a great game to play, but it's not worth spending the whole day on. Turn it off soon

and do something else."

"Sure, Dad. In just a minute," Doug called back.

A little later, the doorbell rang. Doug never even looked up. It rang again. This time, Mom thundered down the stairs to answer it. "Doug, didn't you hear the doorbell?" she asked as she reached for the doorknob. "Oh, hi, Nathan. Yes, he's here. Come on in. Doug, it's Nathan."

"Hi, Doug," Nathan called as he plopped down. "Whatcha up to?"

"Playing my Escape From Zoomania game. I'm up to the third level," Doug said. "I already got by the hippo, the rhino, and the moose. Look, I'll show you."

"No, thanks," Nathan said as he stood up. "All that video-game stuff gets boring after a while. You wanna play catch? Or build a castle with your big blocks? Or something?"

Doug shook his head. Right now, all he wanted to do was play his video game. "Maybe in just a minute. I've got to beat this level." He didn't even notice that Nathan waited around for a few minutes and then left.

"Now, up the tree," he muttered to his character on the screen as he pushed the buttons. Suddenly, a big basket of laundry fell in front of him.

"Doug, are you still playing that game? Turn it off and go play outside."

"Just a minute, Mom," Doug said, leaning around her to see the screen. "I just have to get by these two hyenas. Then I can escape from this level."

Mom looked at her watch. "You've been here all day. What happened to Nathan?"

Doug brushed at her like he was trying to chase off a mosquito. "I don't know. I guess he left."

Mom put her hands on her hips. "Then I want to see you doing something else. You've played this game long enough for one day."

She reached down and turned it off.

"Mom! You can't do that!" Doug tried to reach past her to turn it back on.

"I believe I can," she added. "Now, get up from here and find something else to do."

Doug slammed down the controller. "Why are you being so mean to me?" he shouted. "I was about to win!"

Mom's eyes got big for a second. Then she squinted them narrow. "What you are about to do is lose this game permanently. Right now, I want you to march straight to your room and sit there until you think of something else to do."

Doug was so angry he was almost in tears. "I don't want to play anything else." He moved over next to the TV. "Just let me play for a few more minutes," he said. "Then I promise I'll stop." He reached to turn it on.

Mom held up two fingers in front of his nose. "Douglas, you may either think of something else to do, or you may sit in your room and stare at the walls. Your choice. Whichever, you're not playing this game for two hours."

Doug opened his mouth but clamped it shut before any words came out. Then he turned and stomped to his room. The door slammed behind him.

Too Much of a Good Thing

Grrrumble!

The scowl on Doug's face was almost as dark as the clouds off in the distance. The distant sound of thunder matched his mood exactly.

If I can't play video games, I'm not doing anything, he promised himself. He just stared at the ceiling.

But not for long. It was too boring. Doug walked over to his desk and opened the drawer that held his baseball cards. Without really thinking about it, he began shuffling through the cards and rearranging them.

I'll just spread these out and put them in order, he thought as he carried them toward the bed. Then he stopped. *No, I don't want to look at my baseball cards. I want to play Zoomania.*

He lay back down on the bed and tried to picture the game in his mind. *If I hide from the gorilla in the reptile house, can I get out before the snakes catch me?* He was still thinking

Playing video, Computer games

of new things to try in the game, when there was a knock at his door.

"Doug, may I come in?" It was his dad.

"Sure," Doug mumbled. He lay there with his eyes closed until he felt someone sit beside him.

"Doug, do you remember that time we were at Grandma's house and she let you have as much ice cream as you wanted?"

Doug's lip curled up. "I remember. It was that green mint kind." He shuddered. "I still can't stand it."

"But you liked it that day," Dad reminded him. "If I remember, you ate the whole carton all by yourself."

Doug remembered too. "And threw it all back up."

"What do you think made you sick that day?" Dad asked. "You've had lots of ice cream since then without getting sick."

Doug frowned. "I guess I ate too much of it."

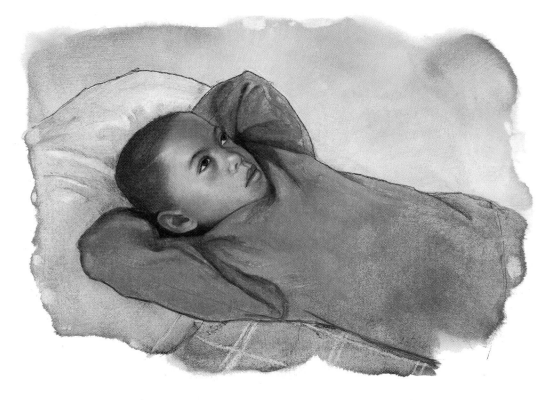

Dad opened his mouth, but before he could say anything, Doug interrupted.

"I know, I know. Too much of even a good thing can be bad. But playing video games won't make me throw up."

Dad raised both hands. "That's good to know. Let me ask you a different question. What if all you ever wanted to do was play baseball?"

"I guess I'd play baseball."

Dad laughed. "Knowing you, you'd play it every day. Before school, after school, during the summer. While other kids were playing basketball or football, you'd just play baseball. How would that change your life?"

Doug thought. "I'd get better at it. I guess I'd make friends with other kids who liked to play it all the time."

"Would you stop being friends with people who didn't play baseball?"

"Probably," Doug admitted. "I wouldn't have time to play anything else with them."

Dad agreed. "And you'd have to stop doing any of the other things you thought were fun. No more bicycle riding, swimming, or playing the trumpet."

Doug was quiet for a second. "I get it. You think if I want to play video games all the time, I'll lose my friends and give up the other things I like to do. But that won't happen."

Dad stared at him. "Are you sure?"

Just then, a gust of wind blew big raindrops against the window. Dad smiled. "I knew if I waited long enough, I could get out of mowing. Doug, I want you to think about what we said here. And about how you've been acting for the last few days."

"Can't I play Zoomania while I think?"

Dad smiled. "Two hours isn't up yet." Then he left.

Doug rolled over and stared out at the storm. Now the rain was coming down in sheets, and the wind was howling through the trees. "Like I could find something else to do in this weather," he grumbled to himself.

Playing video games doesn't make me sick, he told himself. *But I did get angry with Mom. I don't usually do that.*

He rolled over and thought some more. *I wouldn't lose any friends just to play video games.* Then he remembered Nathan. *I guess I haven't played with Nathan much for the last few days. Is he looking for new friends who aren't always playing video games?*

With a loud knock, Mom's head appeared at the door. "Two hours are up. You can come out and play whatever you want."

Doug was still feeling a little angry. "It's about time," he muttered. He settled in front of the game again. Just as the Zoomania sign lighted up, every light in the house went out.

"Hey!" he said as the game disappeared. "What happened?"

Dad came out and flicked the light switch. "The electricity is out. I guess the storm must have knocked down some wires. It may take a few hours to repair. I'd better find the candles."

"Perfect," Doug said. "Just perfect. First, I can't play for two hours. Then I can't play for the rest of the day. This is so boring." He just sat there for a while.

The storm began to move away, and voices from the kitchen carried out to where he sat. "Ooh, look at that! It's beautiful."

Doug had to go see. His mom and dad were staring out the door. "Oh, it's a rainbow. That is great." He moved out into the yard to see it better. The last few sprinkles spattered around him as he walked down the sidewalk.

What is that sound? he asked himself as he got closer to the street. *It sounds like a river.*

Then he saw it. It was kind of a river. The runoff of the heavy rain was rushing down the gutters on both sides of the street.

"Hey, Doug!" Nathan waved from next door. "Come on over. We'll race stick boats from my driveway to yours."

Doug took a deep breath. "OK, I'll be right there." Then he turned and ran back to his house. He yanked the kitchen door open, almost pulling his mother out into the yard.

"Whoa!" she said.

"Sorry, Mom," Doug said. "And I'm sorry about how I acted earlier."

"You're forgiven," she said with a kiss and a hug. "Now go have fun."

"Call me when the electricity comes back on," he called over his shoulder.

The stickboats raced again and again. "Go, go!" Doug shouted to his boat. "Faster, faster!"

Before long, his mom stuck her head out of the doorway. "Doug, you can come in now. The electricity is back on."

"Just a minute, Mom!"

Too Much of a Good Thing

BLOWOUT

Hey, Colin!" Jason shouted down the hall as he shouldered his way through the jabbering crowd toward Colin's locker. *I hope this is a good idea,* Jason thought. *I don't want Colin to think I'm weird.*

"Hey, Colin, what are you doing Saturday night?"

Colin leaned against his locker door. "Nothing, probably. Why?"

"My brother Jeff's going to be home from college. He's taking his girlfriend to a concert at the coliseum. He's got two extra tickets—you wanna tag along?"

"Sounds great!" Colin's eyes lighted up. "Who's playing?"

"I don't think you've heard of them. They're called Wise Man Rock. Jeff heard them at college, and he says they're great."

Then came the hard part. Jason knew that Colin's family didn't go to church or anything. *He might think going a Christian concert is really dumb,* Jason thought. So he cleared

Prayer; witnessing to others

his throat and added, "I think they're a, er, contemporary Christian group."

Colin slammed the locker door. Then he smiled. "Hey, it's better than staying home and watching TV. I'll ask my mom."

That wasn't too bad, Jason decided on the way home. *Maybe the Christian thing won't come up at all.* Then he felt bad for thinking that way. *I like being a Christian, but talking to other people about it really makes me nervous.*

Saturday night, Jason slid into the back seat of his mom's old station wagon behind Jeff and his girlfriend, Sandy. "Now be careful," Mom reminded. "I told Colin's mother that you'd drive safely, Jeff. You know how bad the traffic can be on Highway 55—especially those big trucks."

"Hey, thanks for taking me along," Colin said when they picked him up.

"Glad you could come," Jeff said. When the car didn't start moving, Jason glanced up to see why. Jeff was reaching for Sandy's hand, and they were bowing their heads.

Oh no! Jason thought in a panic. *Jeff's going to pray before we start.* It never bothered him before when Jeff prayed before leaving on a drive. But now . . . *Colin's going to think we're total religious fanatics.*

Jeff began to pray. "Lord, we ask for Your protection tonight as we travel to the concert. Amen."

Colin was silent for a few moments, and Jason tried to think of some excuse for his brother. Then Colin asked, "Jeff, what are you taking in college?" Just as if nothing weird had happened.

Jeff answered as he pulled out onto Highway 55. "I'm taking chemical engineering. I'd like to find a way to make better fuel—something less dangerous than the gas that guy's hauling."

The silver gasoline tanker passed slowly by in the left lane, followed by two more eighteen-wheel trucks. "This highway is like a racetrack," Sandy said. "Keep your eyes on the road, Jeff."

"How can I, when you're so beautiful?" Jeff asked, batting his eyelashes. Sandy smiled. Jason and Colin made gagging noises.

Before long, everyone began to talk about music, especially the concert at the coliseum. "Wise Man Rock has a great album out," Jeff said. "I want to . . ."

Blammm!

The explosive sound blew everything else out of Jason's mind. Immediately, the station wagon headed toward a deep ditch on the right side of the road. Jason could only stare as Jeff turned with all his might. The car swung away from the ditch!

But it skidded across two lanes. "Hold on, everyone!"

Sandy screamed. The car was skidding sideways down the middle of the highway.

Jason could hear scraping metal and see red sparks flying up. *We're going over!* he screamed silently. *The car's going to roll!*

Then, before he could think another thought, the car came to a complete stop, sideways across the two center lanes. Jeff didn't waste any time. "Get out of the car—now!"

Jason jumped out and raced right behind Colin to the side of the highway. "Is everyone OK?" Jeff asked, panting.

"I'm all right," Colin said. Jason nodded.

But something wasn't right. It was too quiet! In the dis-

tance to their right, they could see little dots of light—headlights of oncoming cars. In the other direction, the little red taillights seemed far away.

"What happened to the traffic?" Jason asked out loud.

"Stay here," Jeff commanded, running out to the car. He yanked the front door open and started pushing.

The old station wagon moved slowly at first, but finally Jeff rolled it to the side of the highway. Immediately, it seemed, a truck roared by. Then every lane was packed with speeding vehicles.

"We had a blowout!" Jeff yelled above the noise. He pointed to the right front wheel. "I must have hit something," Jeff said, shaking his head. Then he added, "God answered our prayer, though. He protected us from the other traffic when we were sliding."

Sandy shivered as another truck whipped by. "It's just amazing that there wasn't a single truck or car nearby until you got the car off the road."

A few minutes later, Jeff had the spare tire on and the car back on four wheels. When he climbed back into the driver's seat, he paused for a moment. "Let's thank God for His protection. Father, thank You for keeping us safe."

Out of the corner of his eye, Jason noticed that Colin bowed his head. *Maybe he won't think we're crazy after all,* he thought.

Colin seemed to have a good time at the concert, and he didn't mention anything about all the praying. Still, the more Jason thought about it, the more he was sure that Colin would be mad at him. Or worse, laugh at him.

Monday morning, Jason walked into the classroom. "There he is," Colin called from across the room. "Jason, tell them about our blowout."

"Well, I—"

Colin couldn't wait for Jason. "The tire blew, and the car was skidding back and forth across the highway. Jeff stopped it, but if there had been any traffic, we would have been smashed for sure. Right, Jason?"

"Uh, right," Jason said.

Colin kept talking. "It was a miracle. Jeff prayed, and God kept us from getting killed. Amazing, right, Jason? But you're probably used to that kind of thing, being a Christian."

"Well, yeah, I guess," Jason answered. He wasn't sure what to say.

"And that Wise Man Rock group was great!"

Jason listened while Colin told the others about the concert. *I guess being a Christian and telling other people about it isn't so weird after all,* he decided. *In fact, I guess it's kind of great!*

Firefighter Dad

I had just put the last plate in the dishwasher when the phone rang. I grabbed it with one soapy hand. "Hello? Just a minute." I held the phone out to Dad. "It's Mr. Martinez, from the fire station."

He wiped off his hands and the phone before he took it. "Hello, Tom. Another one? That sounds bad. OK, I'll be ready in the morning."

"Where's the fire this time, Dad?" I asked when he hung up.

"In the mountains up north. They need our help out there for a few days." We finished the dishes while he explained.

"You'll whip it," I said as I started the dishwasher. "You always do." I was so proud of my dad. Besides his real job in town, he was a firefighter pilot.

Dealing with death, guilt

Sometimes, he would fly in the smoke jumpers. They would parachute out to fight the forest fires that were far from any roads. Sometimes, my dad would fly the planes that dumped fire retardant from the sky.

"Katherine," my mom called from the other room, "is your field trip tomorrow? Do I need to send some extra money?"

"No," I answered, "the trip is next week. Tomorrow we have our science test." As soon as I said it, I remembered. "Oh no! Our science test is tomorrow!"

"Katherine, didn't we ask you if all your homework was done?" Mom looked disappointed. "Now it's time for bed."

I got a strange feeling in my stomach, like I always do when something is wrong. It felt like caterpillars in tennis shoes were walking in circles.

"But, Mom, I forgot! And I have to study, or I'll never remember those new vocabulary words."

Dad spoke up. "You get ready for bed. I'll come in and help you study for a few minutes before we turn off the light."

It only took a few minutes to go over the science words. Then Dad turned off my light. "You have to leave in the morning to put out that fire?" I asked.

He sat on the side of my bed and pushed my hair back with his fingers. "I'll be gone bright and early," he said in the dark. "Now you need to go to sleep."

"OK," I answered with a hug, "but put it out in a hurry. I want you home soon! Will you tell me goodbye in the morning?"

"I will," he promised. "But will you wake up when I do it?" We both laughed. Everyone knows how hard it is to wake me up.

"I'll wake up," I promised. But I didn't. I can barely remember someone shaking me. I grumbled and rolled over.

Only a few days later, I was working to get out of school. "Please, Mom," I whined. "I'd learn just as much at Seaside City as I would at school. Can't I go with you?"

I didn't really think my mom would let me go. With Dad gone and Aunt Elisabeth visiting, Mom wouldn't want to worry with me or my sister. But a trip to Seaside City was worth begging for. If you like dolphins, whales, and water shows as much as I do, you would have begged too.

"No, Katherine. You've missed enough school this year. And your voice lessons are this afternoon. Your father should be home tomorrow. This weekend, we'll all go and spend a day at Seaside City."

With that argument lost, it sounded like I was in for just another normal, boring school day. You don't know how much I wish it had been just that.

"Come on, Sarah," I grumped to my sister. "Let's go."

My frown didn't last long. "My dad's coming home tomorrow," I told Kim and Cindy as soon as I saw them. "I can't wait!"

Dad was gone a lot during fire season, but when he was home, it was party time! He took us to places like Seaside City, amusement parks, and the zoo. He taught us to skate, canoe, and water-ski.

But the thing he did best was sing. People in our church loved him. "Your father sings so beautifully," they would say. "God gave him a wonderful voice."

Even better, they said to me, "I can tell whose daughter you are, just by looking at you."

I felt so proud when they said that! I was already taking voice lessons so I could sing like him. My friends, Kim and

Cindy, were taking lessons too, so we practiced together.

School started off like normal. First was spelling, then language, then social studies.

"Psst! What country are you working on?" Kim whispered across the aisle. We were supposed to be finishing our social studies reports.

"Brazil," I answered. "It's all about the Amazon River and rain forests and stuff."

"Hey, who's that stranger?" Kim whispered, pointing to the front of the room. A woman was bent over Mrs. Towson's desk, talking quietly to her.

"That's no stranger. That's my Aunt Elisabeth," I said. "Great! Maybe Mom changed her mind, and I get to go to

Seaside City after all."

"Katherine," Aunt Elisabeth said softly, "get your things.

Let's go." With a big grin at Kim, I dashed to the door. Mrs. Towson gave me a strange look, but I didn't slow down.

"Do I get to go to Seaside City?" I asked, skipping beside Aunt Elisabeth.

She didn't answer. I got that strange feeling, like those caterpillars in tennis shoes were walking in my stomach.

"What's going on?"

She didn't answer. "Where do we go to get your sister?" she asked. I pointed, and nothing else was said.

The caterpillars in my stomach started racing.

"It's My Fault"

All the way home, no one said a word. I plastered my face to the window and watched as the cars raced by. Everything seemed the same, but something was wrong. Very wrong.

By the time we turned onto our street, the caterpillars were wearing boots. And stomping.

We had to park on the other side of the street because of all the cars. I hung back and let Sarah go into the house first. People were everywhere. And they were all crying. Sarah started crying too.

A woman from our church put her arms around me and cried. "He was such a good daddy."

I pushed her away. "Mom? Mom!" She was sitting on the couch, just like she had that morning when she brushed my hair. But nothing else was the same. As soon as she looked at me, I knew.

Daddy wasn't coming home tomorrow. He wasn't ever

Dealing with death; guilt

coming home again.

I pushed past another person and rushed to my mother. She pulled Sarah and me close to her and cried while someone else explained.

"The firefighters say that he was trying to put out the last big hot spot. He told them, 'Let's smother this fire and go home.' He got one more load of retardant, and flew right over the flames. But something went wrong, and the plane crashed."

Just like that, he was gone. I didn't have a father anymore.

For a while, I just sat there while everyone else cried. I didn't feel anything but those awful caterpillars in my stomach. More people kept coming in. Suddenly, I was about to explode. I couldn't stand all those people another second. "I'm going for a walk," I said as I jumped up and headed for the door. I yanked it open right in front of Kim and her mother.

"Let's go," I said, grabbing Kim's arm. "I have to get out of here."

We went down to the park, like we had a thousand times before. "How did you get out of school early?" I asked.

"My mom came and got me after she heard about . . . what happened," Kim answered as we got on the swings. I nodded, and we swung as high as the swings would go.

Kim started talking like she was afraid not to. "Robert brought a frog for science class, like the one in our book, you know? And it got loose and jumped off the table! Mrs. Towson was so scared she screamed and jumped up on her chair!"

I laughed so hard I almost fell out of the swing.

"I shouldn't be laughing," I said a few minutes later, letting the swing coast to a stop. "My father just died."

Kim stopped too. "Your dad liked to laugh. He always laughed with us when we told dumb jokes. I think he'd want you to keep laughing. At least sometimes." She looked at her watch. "I'd better get back. My mom's probably looking for me. It's almost time for our voice lessons. I guess you're not going today."

"Why not?" I asked. We went back to the house. It was still full of crying people. "Mom, I'm going to my voice lesson with Kim," I whispered in her ear as I hugged her.

"Are you sure you feel like it?" she asked.

"I'll feel better away from all these people," I answered. She smiled her OK, and I left.

Cindy looked really surprised to see me. I guess everyone had heard about the crash by now. "Are you sure you want to practice?" she asked.

"I'm fine," I said. And I was. For a few minutes.

We sang several songs. Then my teacher picked one I'd heard my dad sing many times. When the music started, I could almost see him up in front of the church, singing.

Suddenly, the caterpillars were back. I would never hear him sing that song again. I would never hear him sing any song again.

I felt a big lump swelling up in my throat. When it was my turn to sing, I couldn't do it. The tears I had held back all day ran down my face. The teacher took one look and handed me the tissue box. I grabbed it and ran out the door.

Outside by a big tree, I cried and cried. I kept thinking, *Why did this happen? Why did God let him die? I need him!*

Suddenly, I stopped. *What if all this is my fault? I told him to put the fire out quickly—maybe he was flying into the danger-ous part of the fire because he was trying to put it out fast. What if it's my fault Daddy died?*

Kim and her mother came out to take me to their car. I

didn't say a word. All the way home I thought, *They wouldn't even drive me home if they knew that it was my fault. They would hate me—everyone would hate me.*

Just before we drove up to my house, an even worse thought hit me. *If Mom finds out, she'll hate me too!*

The caterpillars felt as big as cows.

The other cars were gone when we drove up, and the house seemed quiet. I ran to the front door without saying goodbye. Mom opened it when she saw me coming.

"Katherine, are you OK?" I nodded with my head down. Kim's mother came up behind me, so I stepped past Mom and ran to my room.

I changed into my pajamas and crawled into bed. By the time Mom came in a few minutes later, my light was out, and I was pretending to be asleep.

She sat on my bed and rubbed my back for a few minutes, then left without saying anything.

She must know that it's my fault, I thought. *She won't want me around anymore.* Without even opening my eyes, I started planning to run away.

It's hard to go to sleep while you're crying and caterpillars are racing in your stomach, but I finally did.

Saying Goodbye

Have you ever awakened from a bad dream, happy that it was just a dream and that it was over? When I first opened my eyes the next morning, I smiled, thinking the bad dream was over. Suddenly, I remembered that it hadn't been a dream. Then they hit me again—the caterpillars started a parade in my stomach.

My father was dead. And it was my fault.

Just a few hours ago, I thought, *my biggest problem was not getting to go to Seaside City. Now everything is different. Everything is a problem.*

I jumped out of bed and pulled my backpack out of the closet. I started stuffing in my favorite clothes and tried to come up with a plan. *I can't go to Kim's or Cindy's—they'll know what I did. Maybe I'll go to Seaside City and work picking up trash like those other kids I've seen. Yeah, I could eat at the concession stands and sneak in behind the otter house to sleep at night.*

Dealing with death; guilt

I was so busy thinking up my plans that I didn't hear Mom come into my room. I don't know how long she stood there, but when she spoke, I jumped.

"Are you going somewhere?" she asked.

My hand flew up to cover my mouth just before I screamed. "Oh, Mom, I . . . uh, no, well . . ." Suddenly, I was crying. "I have to leave!"

Tears came to her eyes, and she came close to hug me. I backed away. "You don't understand! It's my fault! I made him promise to put the fire out in a hurry. That's what he was trying to do when the plane crashed. It's my fault Daddy's dead!"

Mom caught me before I could back away. She let me cry for a minute, then took my face in her hands. "Katherine, it is not your fault. Fighting fires is a dangerous job. Daddy was being as careful as he could. He wouldn't have hurried if that made the danger worse. His crash was an accident. It didn't have anything to do with his promise to you."

For once, the caterpillars stopped. "Are you sure?" I asked, looking up to be certain she meant it.

"Completely sure," she answered. "Now, promise me you'll never run away. I need you now more than ever."

I promised her with my biggest hug.

"I need to go and make plans for the funeral," she said while I squeezed her. "Do you want to go with me?"

I latched onto her hand like I was never going to let go again.

Later I asked, "Do we have to have a funeral? It will just be a bunch of people standing around crying. That makes me crazy! I just want this to be over."

Mom said, "A funeral is an important part of grieving, of feeling sad and saying goodbye."

"But I don't want to say goodbye," I whispered. Then I remembered something. "Daddy didn't tell me goodbye. The night before he left, he promised to wake me up and say good-bye the next morning. But he didn't."

Mom smiled. "Yes, he did. I woke up and ate breakfast with him. Before he left, he went into your room and called your name. You rolled over and grunted. He patted your shoulder and said, 'Goodbye, sweetheart. I love you too.'"

"Really?" That gave me a nice kind of tingling feeling inside. Almost like when Daddy hugged me. "I wish I had been awake. At least he knew that I loved him."

The sad and scared caterpillar kind of feeling came back and stayed with me all through the funeral. In the next week, it would go away for a while, but then something would happen to bring it back.

One day, just before recess, Mrs. Towson reminded us about the field trip. Kim asked, "Do you want to ride with me and my mom?"

"No," I answered, "my dad said that he would . . ." I stopped, and my shoulders slumped. "No, I guess he won't." I sat with my head on my desk all during recess.

Then on another night, I walked into the kitchen with my

science book in one hand. "Mom, can you or Dad help me study—" I stopped, but the word was already out. I dropped the book and ran to my room.

Mom followed me, and we cried together for a few minutes. "You miss him a lot, don't you?" she asked.

I sniffed and nodded. "What will I do without a father?" I asked, with my arms around her neck.

She held me tight. "You still have a Father. Your Father in heaven is still with you. He knows what has happened. He loves you very much. You'll have to learn to depend on His love and protection."

I didn't really understand what she meant then. But I understand a little more now. If God is really full of love and fun like my dad, then I know it's OK to be happy. And I know that God is always worrying about me and taking care of me.

I'll always miss my dad, but knowing my heavenly Father is there keeps the caterpillars from taking over.

Saying Goodbye

Snake Heads and Slimy Tongues

7

You don't know how tired I was of that hospital. "When are we taking Joey home?" I asked Mom. She turned and smiled. "We'd love to bring him home today. But the doctors say he's not strong enough yet."

"Is he getting better?" Don't tell anyone, but I really missed him. Our room was too quiet.

"The doctors say he is better now," Dad answered. "But he's very weak. He needs to decide to get well. That's why we're going to the Animal Park Safari today. Joey needs to get excited, have some fun, and want to get out of this hospital."

The window beside me buzzed up, then down as I pushed the button. "So all I need to do is make him laugh? No problem."

"I hope so," Dad said as he parked. "Close your window, and let's go get him."

But my window wouldn't go up. "Dad, it's stuck again."

Dealing with sickness; laughter

He tried pushing his button, but nothing happened. "Well, leave it. Let's go."

I waited in the hospital lobby until Mom and Dad brought Joey rolling up in a wheelchair. He looked too pale and too skinny. "Hey, Joey," I called. "Are you ready to go round up some wild animals?"

Joey shrugged. "I guess," was all he said.

"Look," I said when they got him settled on his side of the back seat, "my window won't go up at all."

Then Dad started the car, and it went up all by itself. "OK, I was wrong!" I said. Joey just stared at me like I was speaking Chinese.

All the way there, I tried my best jokes. He almost smiled once. At the park office, the ranger gave us bags of corn to feed the animals along the way. "You can leave your windows open and feed the animals," she said. "But don't get out of your car."

"Can the animals get in the car with us?" I asked, trying to be funny. No one laughed, so I tried again as we drove away.

"Corn?" I said. "What kind of wild animals are out here, chickens?" Joey didn't even crack a smile.

This isn't working at all, I thought as we drove in. *Joey hasn't laughed even once.*

"Look, there's a deer," Dad said, pointing ahead. "Wait a minute There are a lot of them."

"Whoa," I whispered. From all around us, deer appeared out of the woods. And I mean all around us. "We're surrounded!" I pushed the button, and my window buzzed down. Three deer put their heads where the window used to be.

"Daniel, they're begging for food," Mom said. "Give them some corn."

Three tongues quickly slurped up the handful of corn I offered. "Hey, that was great," I said, looking over at Joey.

"Great," he said quietly.

Dad drove on slowly. I watched Joey as much as I did the goats we saw next. He looked like someone who was watching reruns—bored and sleepy, with his eyes about half closed.

"Look!" Mom said suddenly, "zebras, ostriches, and a giraffe!" We stopped behind a car that was almost hidden behind a sea of legs and bodies.

"Oh, look," Mom said, "that giraffe is sticking its head right down to their window. It's eating out of their hands!"

When I saw Joey lean forward with his eyes wide open, I knew what I had to do.

I unsnapped my seat-belt and leaned out the window as far as I could. "Come and get it!" I called, waving the bag. "Free corn to everyone with a long, slimy tongue!"

"Daniel, get back inside this car," Mom demanded.

I sat down and grinned at Joey. "That ought to bring them running." I didn't know how right I was until I saw his eyes look past me, then get really big.

When I turned around, two ostriches were staring me right in the face. Have you ever seen an ostrich up close? Let me tell you, they may have beautiful feathers, but their faces are ugly!

With those long, skinny necks and the ugly, round faces, they made me think of snakes with beaks.

"Here," I said as I held up a handful of corn, "have a snack."

Smack! Smack-smack! One of them grabbed at the corn in my right hand, pounding on my palm like a hammer. The other snake head was grabbing at the bag of corn in my left hand. "Hey!" I shouted, "get back!"

"Roll up your window," Mom suggested, leaning away from the birds. Since most of the corn from my right hand had either been swallowed or scattered, I stabbed the window but-

Snake Heads and Slimy Tongues

ton to close them out.

Nothing happened.

Well, that's not true. Plenty was happening. Now both of them were snatching at the bag of corn in my left hand. "Dad! My window's stuck again! Drive away!"

Dad was trying not to laugh. "I can't. We're stuck in traffic. Just keep the bag away from them, and they'll leave."

I tried. I leaned away from the window. They leaned farther in. I covered the bag with both hands. They pounded so hard I dropped the bag into my lap.

Just try to imagine what happened next.

In half a second, both ostriches were jabbing full force at the bag—in my lap. "Hey! Help!"

Mom and Dad helped by laughing even harder. Finally, one snake head snagged the bag and jerked up. Corn flew all over the car. I just knew both birds were going to be in my lap next, scrounging for the corn.

I got mad. "That's it!" I shouted. I slapped the nearest long neck and banged the other bird right on the head. "Get out! Get out!"

I kept slapping and shoving until both snake heads were outside the car. They headed for the car behind us.

"Thanks a lot," I said as I wiped corn and ostrich slobber off my shirt. "I could have been eaten alive." Mom tried to answer, but she could only make cackling sounds.

Then I heard another laugh—from the seat beside me.

"Ha-ha!" Joey was laughing so hard he could barely talk. "The look on your face when you dropped that bag, and they, they —" He couldn't finish.

I started to get mad, just like I always did when Joey laughed at me. Then I saw the tears in my mother's eyes. And

I knew they were from more than laughter.

"Oh, yeah!" I crowed. "I showed those snake heads a thing or two! Come on back here," I shouted out the window. "Come back and fight like a bird!"

Joey kept laughing. Mom kept smiling. And I kept feeling like, finally, everything was going to be OK.

Then the giraffe stuck its head in my window. Have you ever been six inches away from a giraffe's tongue? Trust me—you wouldn't like it.

But that's another story . . .

A Perfect Smile

As soon as she stepped on the Camp Killdeer ski boat, Lindsay knew what she wanted. Even more than she wanted to learn how to ski, she wanted to be just like Nicole.

Lindsay stared as the counselor turned and smiled her perfect smile. *I wish I was as pretty as Nicole. With this job, she must be the most popular girl around,* Lindsay thought.

Nicole was the junior counselor for the Blue Jay cabin and a skiing instructor. *I wish I were in the Blue Jay cabin,* Lindsay thought. *Instead, I'm stuck in the Osprey cabin with Mandy, the kitchen janitor.*

Mandy seemed like a nice person, but she was so . . . plain and boring! Not glamorous and popular like Nicole.

Nicole sat near the front of the boat, her

Influence of older kids; being thoughtful

swimsuit covered by a bright blue Camp Killdeer shirt. When Nicole began rubbing sunscreen on her arms, Lindsay pulled out her bottle and did the same.

"Hey, Nicole," a girl called from the back, "can I borrow your sunscreen? I left mine back at the cabin."

"I don't think so," Nicole called back. "This stuff is expensive." She slipped her sunglasses on and leaned back.

Lindsay put on her sunglasses too.

Nicole showed everyone the basics of skiing, then stayed in the water as each girl took a turn trying.

"Remember, bend your legs and keep your arms straight," Nicole told Amy, one of the girls from the Osprey cabin. "Ready?" She turned to

the driver and said, "Hit it!"

Amy rose up from the water and wobbled along for ten seconds before she fell. "That's a good start," Nicole called. "Who's next?"

Lindsay was the last one to try. Nicole helped her get the skis on her feet. When she was ready, Nicole shouted, "Hit it!" Lindsay tensed up and flopped right over onto her face.

She came up sputtering. "One more time," Nicole said as she helped Lindsay get set again. "Remember to lean back."

It was an instant replay of the first try. When Lindsay popped back up, Nicole was reaching for her skis. "That's enough for one day," she said. "Let's head in."

On the way back, Lindsay found a place near Nicole. "Do you think I'll ever learn?" she asked.

"We'll keep trying," Nicole answered with her perfect smile. "It's really not that hard."

That afternoon, Lindsay went swimming. After a few minutes in the water, she lay down on her towel.

"Hi, Lindsay." Amy and several of the other Ospreys walked up. "We just got here," Amy said. "Can we leave our towels and stuff here while we swim?"

Lindsay tried to imagine what Nicole would say. "I guess so," she answered.

The girls dropped their towels, and Amy opened her bag. "Oh no! I forgot to pack my sunscreen." She looked around. "Lindsay, can I borrow yours?"

Lindsay knew the answer to that one. "I don't think so," she said. "You should have your own. Go buy some at the camp store."

Amy stepped back. "Well, I'm sorry I asked. Come on, girls." With a huff, they gathered their things and stalked away. Lindsay leaned back and practiced her smile.

Later, at the camp store, Lindsay saw a Camp Killdeer shirt like Nicole had. "I'll take this," she told the clerk. *It took almost all my money,* she thought, *but it's worth it.*

When she stepped out of the food line in the cafeteria that night, Lindsay looked around for Nicole.

"The camp shirt looks great on you," someone behind her said. Lindsay whirled around, almost spilling her milk. It was Mandy, wearing a stained apron and holding a mop. "Sorry, I didn't mean to scare you. Can I carry the glass to your table?"

"Uh, thanks," Lindsay stammered. She led the way to a table near the back wall. "See you later." Mandy waved and went back to her mopping.

Nicole sat nearby with a group of junior counselors. She was wearing her blue shirt. Lindsay hoped Nicole would notice that their shirts matched.

She didn't. As she and her friends walked past Lindsay, someone said, "Hey, let's go back down to the beach."

"I don't think so," Nicole answered. "I'm going to wash my hair before campfire."

On the way back to her cabin, Lindsay practiced her new favorite saying. "I don't think so." She tried to sound like Nicole. "I don't think so."

There was talking and laughing in the Osprey cabin as Lindsay walked up. But when she stepped in, it got a lot quieter. *I wonder if they were talking about me,* Lindsay thought. She went quickly to her bunk. *Maybe I'll wash my hair now too.*

She searched through her suitcase. *Oh no! I didn't pack my shampoo. I'll ask someone if I can borrow . . .* She looked around the cabin. *Maybe I'll just rinse it tonight and buy some*

shampoo tomorrow.

She was halfway to the showers before she remembered. *I spent all my money on that blue shirt! Now what will I do?* She trudged on toward the showers, past the Blue Jay cabin.

Maybe Nicole would lend me some shampoo. She walked up to the Blue Jay door but heard voices from inside before she knocked.

"I don't think so. These kids are driving me crazy."

It was Nicole's voice. Lindsay froze and listened.

"They're always whining about something. And clumsy! Some of the kids in my class spent all morning skiing on their faces!"

Lindsay turned and ran from the laughter. With tears in her eyes, she ran past the Osprey cabin to a big tree behind the cafeteria. There she sat, all alone.

"Lindsay? What are you doing here?" It was Mandy, taking out the trash from the kitchen. "Are you OK?"

Lindsay turned her head away. "No, I'm not. I don't have any shampoo. I made all the girls in the cabin mad at me. And people are laughing at me because I can't ski."

Mandy set the trash bags down. "Well, let's see. You can borrow my shampoo. The other Ospreys are really nice—I know they'll forgive you if you ask. And I'll teach you everything I know about skiing, if you want me to."

Lindsay turned and stared at Mandy. "Why are you being so nice to me?"

Mandy sat down beside her. "Lindsay, the reason I work at this camp is because I like kids. I like to help them learn new things like skiing. I like to help them have fun."

"Really?" Lindsay asked. Mandy's smile told her it was true.

The last day of the week, Lindsay came into the cafeteria. "Mandy! I skied all the way around the lake!"

Mandy smiled. "That's great! I knew you would!"

"Lindsay, come sit with us," Amy called from across the room. Lindsay turned and waved, almost knocking the tray out of a girl's hands.

"I'm sorry," Lindsay said with a perfect smile. "Let me carry your glass for you."

Splunkhead

I'm sorry you can't go in the cave with us, Murph," Sierra said as she patted her dog on the head. "But you'll be happy out here by the truck."

Murph whined and batted his tail against the ground. He had already followed Sierra all the way to the end of the rope. "Come on, Angel," her dad called from down the trail.

She patted Murph one more time. "Your water bowl is full. And with all these clouds, you won't get too hot. I have to go now. Dad and Mr. Know-it-all are waiting."

With Murph barking behind her, Sierra ran to catch up with Dad and her cousin Edward. "Does your dog ever stop barking?" Edward asked with a pained look on his face.

"He'll stop when we're out of sight," Dad answered before Sierra could say anything. "Let's get going." He led the way toward a small, dark opening in the side of the hill. "I've only been in Deadman's Cave once before."

"But Mom's been in it a lot, right?" Sierra asked.

Faith in the truth of the Bible

Dad nodded. "Both of your mothers have. Your grandfather owns this land, and I guess he and his kids explored the cave a long time ago. But not many people have been in it in the last few years."

"Why do they call it 'Deadman's Cave'? " Sierra asked.

Dad laughed. "Your mom says they called it that just to scare each other."

Edward rolled his eyes and changed the subject. "These rocks appear to be limestone. That would explain the presence of a cave."

Sierra hated to, but she asked. "How?"

Edward sniffed. "Limestone is easily dissolved by water. Caves are commonly found in limestone hills or mountains."

"Here we go," Dad called as he clicked on his flashlight and ducked in. "You'll have to turn sideways to fit through this first turn."

"Edward doesn't have a sideways," Sierra announced. "He and the backpack are too thick to make it." She pushed past him and slipped into the cave. She turned to watch as Edward slipped the pack off his shoulders and squeezed through. "Why are you carrying that backpack, anyway?" she asked.

"A good spelunker always carries emergency supplies," Edward sniffed.

"Hey, who are you calling a splunkhead?"

Dad interrupted. "Sierra, it's spelunker. That's what you call someone who explores caves. Edward's right. A good cave explorer always comes prepared. What did you bring, Edward?"

Edward shone his light into his pack. "A coil of rope, some bandages, a knife, a canteen of water, some candles, and some matches."

"Very good," Dad replied, slipping on his own small fanny-pack. "I brought some of the same things. Along with a compass. Now, let's get going. There's supposed to be a stream running through the cave. Let's see if we can find it."

Sierra's light flashed from side to side as they moved down the narrow passageway. "Look at that," she said as her light found passageways to the left and to the right. "I wonder where those trails go?"

"The ceiling gets lower here," Dad called from up ahead. "Watch your head."

Bonk!

"Oww!" Sierra moaned. She shined her light up. "I hit my head on . . . a brown icicle?" As she looked up, a drop of water almost fell into her eye.

"That is a stalactite," Edward announced.

"A stalak-what?"

He sighed. "The rocks hanging from the ceiling like icicles are called stalactites. The ones growing up from the floor are stalagmites." He shone his light up on the stalactite just as another drop of water formed and fell with a splat.

"That stalactite is still growing," Edward added. "Every time a drop of water passes over it, it grows a little longer. It's probably been here for a million years. In another million, it might reach the floor."

Sierra pointed her light at her dad. "A millions years? Is he right?"

Dad shrugged. "That is what most scientists think."

Edward pointed back at the stalactite. "It's simple. Every time a drop of water passes over the rock formation, it leaves behind a tiny bit of the minerals it carries. Slowly, those minerals build up on the surfaces. So, with every

drop, the stalactite grows a little longer."

Sierra rolled her eyes. "So?"

"So this stalactite has grown one drip at a time for thousands and thousands of years." With that, Edward flipped his light around and headed down the trail like there was nothing else to be said.

Sierra wasn't so sure. She followed, but she asked, "Dad, at church I learned that God created the world only a few thousand years ago. And that there was a flood that covered the whole world and made it into what we see now. How can that be true if this cave has been here for a million years?"

Dad scrambled along after them. Before he could answer, Edward spoke up as he squeezed through a narrow space. "You can't argue with scientific facts, Uncle James. Scientists can measure how often the water drips and how many minerals each drop of water leaves. Then they figure how big the stalactite is. The bigger the stalactite, the

longer it's been there."

Dad didn't answer him. Instead, he said, "Sierra, what do we do when Murph wants to come into the house and his feet are muddy?"

Sierra squeezed through before she answered. "Dad! What does that have to do with anything?"

Dad sucked in his stomach as he reached the narrow opening. "Just answer," he said in a high voice. As he reached out for a grip to pull himself through, his flashlight smacked against the wall.

Crack! Blink! The light went out.

"Dad, are you OK?" Sierra stopped and shined her light on him.

"I'm fine," he answered, "but my flashlight is dead. Edward, you didn't pack a spare flashlight bulb, did you?"

"No, I didn't think of that," Edward admitted.

"Well, I guess I'll just have to stick close to you, Sierra." Dad popped out of the narrow place and stood still for a moment. "Does anyone else hear that sound?" he asked.

They all strained to listen. Finally, Sierra heard a rumbling, grumbling sound. It seemed to be coming from somewhere above them. "What is it?"

Not even Mr. Know-it-all had the answer.

Dirty Feet and Danger

The strange rumbling noise died away. "Do you think the stream in the cave could make that noise?" Sierra asked.

"I don't think so," Dad answered. "The stream is still below us somewhere. Let's keep going. Sierra, you didn't answer my question. What do you do with Murph when he's been in the mud?"

Sierra thought about her dog's hairy feet as she followed Edward. "I put him in the bathtub and wash his feet off. Then the tub is coated with mud, and I have to rinse it out."

Dad went on. "What would happen if we never rinsed it out? What if the water always ran out, but not the mud?"

"The mud would get thicker and thicker on the bottom of the tub," Sierra answered as she ducked under the low ceiling.

Dad ducked too. "Right. Now, if you washed the dog's feet every day, how long would it be until the tub was full of mud?"

Faith in the truth of the Bible

"Dad! How would I know?"

"Think about it."

"Well," Sierra said as she thought, "it depends on how dirty his feet are."

"Exactly," Dad said from behind her. "Wait for us up there, Edward. The dirtier Murph's feet are, the faster the tub would

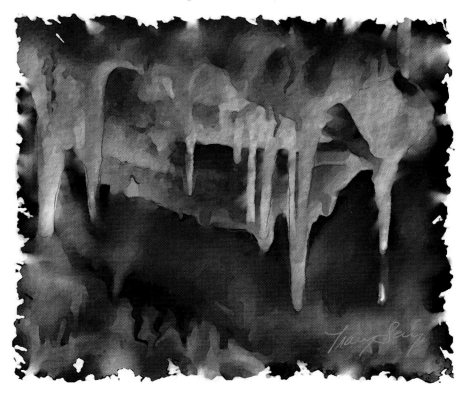

fill with mud. Now, stalactites are formed as the minerals in the water stick while the water drips off. So how long it takes for a stalactite to form depends on . . . "

"I get it!" Sierra interrupted. "The dirtier the water is—I mean, the more minerals and stuff in it—the quicker the stalactites would grow."

"And if there really was a worldwide flood, like the Bible

says, the water would have been muddy and full of minerals. Just right for growing stalactites quickly. So you see, Edward," Dad said as they all stood together, "even when there is scientific evidence, there may be more than one way to look at it."

For once, Edward had nothing to say. Neither did Sierra. She was busy staring at the walls that her flashlight showed. "Wow! This room is bigger than Grandpa's whole house!"

"And there's the stream," Dad said. "Come on, we'll follow it."

Sierra was still staring at the walls. "How did this part of the cave get so big?"

"The water did it," Edward said. "Long ago, that stream was running through a narrow space up where the ceiling is now. Slowly, it washed away the limestone, all the way down to here."

"That would have taken . . . a million years!"

Edward looked at Uncle James. "That's what scientists think."

Dad led the way down to the stream as he spoke. "Like Edward said, limestone dissolves slowly in water."

Sierra was right behind him. "What do you mean? Does it get soft and fall apart like mud?"

"Not exactly. It's more like a lollipop. It just gets smaller and smaller until it's gone. Anyway, as water seeps through the limestone . . ."

Splash! They stepped into the stream. "That's cold," Sierra said. "What do you mean, seeps?"

"The water flows through and around the limestone. It's like your mother's geranium plant on the porch. You turn on the hose and let some water trickle into the pot, and pretty soon, the water is flowing out from the holes in the bottom."

Dirty Feet and Danger

"I get it," Sierra said.

Dad stopped at a stalactite. "This cave was formed the same way. As it rained, water seeped through the limestone and formed underground streams or rivers like this. And as the water slowly dissolved the rock, the space inside got bigger."

"So," Sierra asked, "did it really take a million years to get this big?"

Dad turned to Edward. "If this stream had always been this size, yes. But what if it were bigger? What if water was rushing through here like a flood?"

"It would wash out the limestone more quickly," Edward agreed. He was staring down at the stream.

"So if Noah's flood really happened," Sierra added, "this cave could have washed out in a hurry."

"Uncle James, is the water getting deeper?" Edward asked. "When we stopped, it was up to my ankle. Now it's over my sock."

Sierra watched her dad's face as he stared at the water. Before he even said a word, she was afraid. "It is deeper. Kids, let's head back. Quick!"

Dad grabbed Sierra's hand and rushed her along after Edward. Now the water was almost to her knees. "Dad, what's happening?"

"That rumbling noise we heard earlier must have been

thunder," he said. "It's raining hard out there somewhere, and this stream is going to flood."

"Will the cave fill up with water?" Sierra squeaked.

"It might."

Edward's voice didn't sound much better than Sierra's. "Maybe that's why they call it Deadman's Cave." He slipped on a rock as he tried to step out of the stream into the big room. "I dropped my flashlight!" he cried.

"Leave it and keep going!" Dad commanded. The big room didn't seem so wide now with the stream covering half of it. "Sierra, shine your light so Edward can see, and follow him."

They rushed up the cave trail. Edward yanked off his backpack and slipped through the narrow part without slowing down. Sierra was right behind him.

"Wait," Dad called. Sierra turned the light back. "My fanny pack is caught. I can't get loose, and I can't back up."

"Dad!" Sierra was almost in tears. "What are we going to—Edward! Quick, give me your knife." He had it in her hands in a second. She slit the pack strap, and her dad popped through.

"Thanks," he said. "Now, keep going!" They rushed on, panting and huffing, until they got back to the place where there were three passageways.

"Which way do we go?" Edward called between breaths.

"I don't remember," Dad said. "They all go up."

"Dad!" Sierra's voice was squeaking again. "The flashlight is getting dimmer."

"I have more batteries," Dad started to say. "No, I don't. They were in the fanny pack." They all stared at each other.

"I still have the candles," Edward said in a quiet voice.

"Let's get them before the flashlight goes out," Dad

agreed. They were digging in Edward's pack when Sierra shouted.

"Quiet! I think I heard something."

"Not water, I hope," Edward squeaked, with a glance behind them.

"Shhh!" They listened, and then Sierra heard it for sure.

"Bark! Bark-bark!"

"It's Murph!" she shouted. "And it's coming from . . . the middle passageway. Come on!"

They rushed ahead until the dim light of the flashlight

Dirty Feet and Danger

melted into the gray light of the cave opening. There sat Murph, with the chewed-off end of the rope hanging around his neck.

"Good boy," Sierra said. "Am I glad to see you."

"And hear you," Edward added, patting the dog's head.

"Well, that was quite an adventure," Dad said as they sat down to rest.

"Uncle James, I didn't know that the Bible stories were supported by scientific facts," Edward said. "Is there anything else I should know?"

Sierra opened her mouth but closed it without saying a word.

WHITE-WATER RAPIDS

I f you fall out of the raft, float with your feet facing downstream."

As he listened to the river guide, Adam didn't think so. *If I fall out, I probably won't float at all. He glanced at his mother's face.*

"Isn't this great!" she said with dancing eyes.

"Sure it is, Mom," Adam answered. "It'll be even greater if we live through it."

She laughed. "Adam, you're so funny!"

That's me, he thought, *funny to the end—and this looks like it!*

Out of the corner of his eye, Adam saw a man's arm grab his mother's waist. He jumped . . . then remembered.

Living with divorced parents

"Are you guys ready to brave the rapids?" Glen asked. He wrapped Adam's mom up in a hug.

Adam rolled his eyes. *I have to get used to this guy. But I don't have to like him!*

Adam was used to the idea of his mother dating. But now, she was talking about getting married.

"Load up!" the guide called. Adam followed the two of them to the very front of the raft. *His mom sat beside Glen, so Adam sat in front of them.*

The first stretch of the river was calm and smooth. *This isn't so bad,* Adam thought. Then he saw white water ahead.

"Here we go!" Mom shouted, waving her paddle in the air. Glen laughed out loud.

Adam's eyes followed the twisting path of the water through the rocks. He gripped his paddle so tight his knuckles turned white.

"This is just a small warm-up rapid," the guide called out. "Be ready to paddle when I say . . . Now! Paddle! All front!"

In spite of his fear, Adam reached in and paddled. He braced his feet against the raft ribs like the guide had taught them. Then they hit the rapids.

Splot-splash! The wall of white water smacked against the raft and sprayed Adam right in the face. "Ahh!" He almost dropped the paddle. Then the raft tipped forward as it cleared the wave. Adam tipped forward too. "Whoa!"

Just as quickly, the raft tipped back. Adam fell onto his seat. Over the sound of the other riders' shouts and screams, Adam heard Glen's loud laughter. *He's laughing at me,* Adam thought. *He can tell I'm afraid.*

Another wall of water rose up. *Splot-splash!* This time, Mom and Glen disappeared under the white spray.

"Yahoo!" *Mom shouted as she slid back against Glen.*

"Whoa-ho," Glen added, his voice muffled by her life jacket.

When the raft glided into a quiet bend, the guide suggested, "Feel free to get out and float along. It's nice and cold." Adam and Glen hopped over the side.

"S-so, how do you like it s-so far?" Glen asked, his teeth chattering.

Adam shrugged and shivered. *He just wants me to admit I'm scared,* he thought. "It's not s-so bad—I'm s-still alive."

Glen tried to wrap his arms around himself. "Yeah, s-so far s-so good. Except now I'm freezing to death."

Adam rolled his eyes. "Then w-why are you in the water?"

"Anything to g-get out of that raft," Glen muttered.

What? Adam shook water out of his ears. "W-what did you s-say?"

Glen stared at Adam as if he wasn't sure whether or not to say something. Then he said, "Look, this-s trip wasn't my idea." He took a deep breath and stopped shivering for a second. "This white-water s-stuff scares me to death."

Adam's jaw fell open. "Y-you? S-scared? Ha-ha-ha!"

Glen pushed wet hair out of his eyes. "I only c-came because I didn't w-want you to think I was a w-wimp. Well, now you know."

"N-no, that's not it. I didn't want to t-take this raft trip either. I've been s-scared to death since we got in! I just didn't w-want you to know it."

They both laughed. *Maybe he's not so bad,* Adam thought. Out loud, he said, "As much as I hate that raft, I've got to get out of this water."

Glen agreed. "If we're going to face death, let's do it without shivering." They climbed back in and shared a grin behind Mom's back.

She knew something was going on. "What were you guys doing? Planning to take over the raft?"

Adam snorted. "Yeah, and head for shore."

"OK," the guide called out, "coming up next is the toughest rapid on the river. We call it the 'Buckin' Bronco.'"

"This is gonna be great!" Mom shouted. Adam heard the nervousness in Glen's laugh but didn't turn to look. He was busy trying to find something to hold onto.

"Paddle! All front!" the guide shouted. They headed straight toward a wall of white water that Adam couldn't even see over.

Splot-splash! The raft hit the wall and reared up like a wild stallion. Adam lost his footholds and fell backward.

"Ahhh!" This time, even Mom was screaming—or was that Glen?

The raft crossed the wall and twisted to the left. The front, along with Adam, tilted straight toward the boiling river.

With his feet loose, there was nothing to hold Adam in the raft except his hands. And they were glued to the paddle.

There wasn't enough time to panic. *Maybe I can grab a rock and hold on,* he thought. His hands flew out in front

of him, still latched onto the paddle. He was flying, stretching for a rock.

He didn't make it.

He stopped in midair. And was yanked back into the raft.

"Adam! Are you OK?" Almost before he could think, he was streched accross his mother's lap and the raft was floating on smooth water.

"W-what happened?" Adam asked, suddenly shivering, even though he wasn't in the water. "I thought I was headed to the bottom for sure."

"Glen grabbed your life jacket," his mom explained. "I thought you were both going overboard."

Glen shrugged. "W-we were. But the r-raft tipped back the other way. We j-just got lucky, I guess."

Adam sat up and whispered. "Maybe you got lucky. I got rescued. Thanks. It must have been . . . scary."

Glen shrugged. "What else could I do? Your mother was watching. I wouldn't want her to think I was . . . afraid or anything."

"What is going on with you two?" Mom asked. "Stop keeping secrets."

Adam just laughed. *Maybe we'll tell her. Next time . . .* Suddenly, he was glad there was going to be a next time. For all three of them.

Feathers and Puzzle

Bye, Elena. See you tomorrow."

Elena turned to wave at her friends from school and then walked on alone down her block. She pulled on the straps to her backpack and mumbled to herself.

"My books sure are heavy today. All because of Mrs. Carmichael. I'll never finish all my science homework."

Elena fished for the shoestring looped around her neck under her sweater. She pulled it out and grabbed the shiny key as she walked up to the next-to-the-last gray stone building on Gulliver Street. Her key fit perfectly in the door to Apartment 117.

"Puzzle," she called as she opened the door. "I'm home, Puzzle." As always, Elena pushed the door shut behind her. Then she locked the

Latchkey kids; handling emergencies

doorknob, turned the deadbolt lock, and slipped the golden chain into place.

Before she finished, Puzzle was rubbing her legs and crying for attention. "Hello, Puzzle," Elena said, scratching behind her cat's ear just the way he liked it.

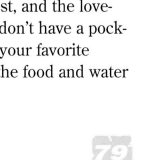

Meow, purrr-purrr. Puzzle rolled over on the black-and-orange spots that gave him his name. He wanted his belly scratched. But Elena patted him once and walked away.

"Feathers, I'm home," she called. But Feathers already knew. She was fluttering and chirping in her cage. *Chir-reep!*

"Hi, Feathers." Elena opened the bird-cage door and reached in. Feathers hopped onto her finger and chirped again. "Time for food and water. Let's go get some."

Elena moved her finger closer to her chest, and the love-bird fluttered over to her shoulder. "Sorry I don't have a pock-et to put you in today. That always has been your favorite place to hide." Elena laughed. She grabbed the food and water

dishes from their places on the cage wires and walked to the kitchen sink. Puzzle padded along behind.

"No, Puzzle, I'm not forgetting you. I'll get your food next."

Elena talked to her pets a lot. They kept her company in the apartment until her mom got home from work. Elena was used to being there with only her pets, but her mom still worried.

"Remember," her mom had said that morning, as she did every morning, "lock the door behind you, and don't open it for anyone."

"Yes, Mother."

"And what do you tell people who call on the phone?"

"My mother can't come to the phone right now. May I take a message?" Elena knew it all by heart.

"And if there is an emergency?"

"Call 9-1-1 for help."

Elena carefully balanced the seed and water containers and walked back to the living room. Feathers fluttered and stuck her head up as Elena reached into the bird cage.

Chir-reep! Feathers said.

"I know," Elena said with a frown. "I need to change the paper in the bottom of your cage. Mom said I had to do it before she gets home." She wrinkled her nose at the dirty job. "I'll do it later."

After eating an orange, watching a couple of cartoon shows, and doing a few minutes of homework, Elena knew she couldn't put it off any longer. "All right, Feathers, let's clean up." Lifting the bird cage off its stand, she set it on the table and unhooked the bottom from the wire sides.

"You wait here," Elena said as she set the top part of the cage on the table. Feathers didn't seem to mind. Then Elena carried the dirty newspaper-covered bottom to the trash can.

"This is gross," she muttered as she dumped it in.

Crash! The loud sound made Elena jump and drop the cage bottom.

"Aaaah!" She was screaming before it even hit the floor. *Someone is trying to break in!* she thought for a second. But not for

much longer.

Before she could even blink, a flurry of feathers and fur rushed past her. Without even looking, Elena knew what had happened. Puzzle had knocked Feathers's cage off the table. And now he was after her!

"Puzzle, stop!" The cat followed the bird into the kitchen

without even slowing down. Elena joined the chase. "Feathers, come here!" Feathers fluttered to a stop on the counter by the sink. But before Elena could get there, Puzzle leapt up toward the bird.

Cheap! Feathers escaped from Puzzle's paws by a feather and headed back out into the living room.

Meow! Puzzle escaped from Elena's hands by a hair and leapt after the bird.

"No!" Elena cried. "Puzzle, come back here!"

Feathers skipped from the table to the back of the couch. Puzzle did the same. Feathers flew to the television, then up to the curtain rod over the window. Puzzle was just one step behind. From the TV, he leapt halfway up the curtain and started climbing, one paw at a time.

"No!"

At that same second, the nails holding the curtain rod pulled out of the wall. Curtain rod, curtain, cat, and bird all fell to the floor.

Elena forgot to scream. For a second, she just stared. Nothing moved under the curtain. "Oh no," she whispered. "Feathers, are you OK?" she almost shouted as she ran to the jumbled pile on the floor.

"Feathers, where are you?" Elena pawed through the curtains until she saw green feathers. "Oh no." Elena picked up her bird. Feathers was still.

"Nothing looks broken." Elena lifted Feathers's wings. Then she got mad. "Puzzle, you are a bad cat. I'm going to . . . Puzzle?"

There, under the curtain rod, was Puzzle. And he wasn't moving, either.

"Oh no! They're both dead!"

Emergency!

"No, no, no," Elena mumbled under her breath as she lifted Feathers's still body up to look at it more closely. "You can't be dead." Then she saw it. The bird's green chest was moving. She was breathing!

"She's alive." Elena lay the bird carefully on the couch and went back to her cat. Kneeling down beside the curtains, she looked carefully at him. He was breathing too!

Elena shook him gently. "Puzzle, wake up!" But the cat just lay there—breathing but not moving.

"What should I do?" Elena asked herself, trying not to cry. "I'm afraid they're both going to die." She tried to think. "I'll call Mom at work." Then she looked at the clock. "I can't call Mom—she's already on her way home."

She paced back to the couch. "I have to do something. This is an emergency!"

Suddenly, Elena knew what to do. She picked up the phone and punched three buttons: 9-1-1.

Latchkey kid; handling emergencies

"Emergency Services," a woman's voice said. "What is the problem?"

"This is an emergency," Elena said with a trembling voice. "I'm afraid they're going to die."

"OK, sweetheart," the operator said, "take it easy. Can you tell me your name and your address?"

"My name is Elena. I live at 1458 Gulliver Street, Apartment 117," Elena recited.

"Elena, are any adults with you?"

"No. My mom isn't home from work yet." Elena could hear the operator talking to other people for a moment. Then she was back.

"OK, Elena. An ambulance is on its way. Luckily, a police car was near your street, so it will be there very soon. Now tell me what happened."

Elena was so worried and afraid she couldn't think very well. She tried to explain. "I don't know why he did it. He's never tried to hurt her before! They've lived here together for a long time."

"What happened? How is she injured?"

"She took off to get away from him. Then the curtain fell. I think the curtain rod hit him on the head." As she spoke, Elena saw something move in the living room. "Wait, he's moving! He's shaking his head! I think he's OK!"

"Who?"

"Puzzle. He was chasing Feathers."

There was silence for a second. Through the window, Elena could see the lights of the police car coming down her street. Somehow, even before the operator said another word, Elena knew she was in trouble.

"Are we talking about your pets?"

Elena wanted to slam down the phone and hide under the table. But it was too late for that. The police car was stopping in front of her house. "Yes," she said quietly. "My bird and my cat. Puzzle was chasing Feathers, and they both got hurt."

"Elena, 9-1-1 is for people emergencies, not animals." Over the phone, Elena could hear the operator talking to someone else. "There is no emergency. Call the ambulance back."

The lights on the police car out on the street snapped off. Elena's voice quivered. "But what about Feathers and Puzzle?"

"Since the officers are already there, they'll come check on you. I'll stay on the phone until they get to your door."

Ding-dong. "That's the officers now. You can open the door."

Elena wasn't so sure. "My mom told me not to open the door for anyone when she's not home."

"And she's exactly right," the woman said, "but we know these are police officers, so it's OK."

Elena hung up and looked through the peephole. Then she turned the locks, unhooked the chain, and opened the door.

"Are you Elena?" one of the two officers asked. She nodded. "I'm Officer Carter, and this is Officer Martinez. Elena, you know you're not supposed to call 9-1-1 unless it's really an emergency, don't you?"

Elena nodded. A tear trickled down her cheek. "She told me that on the phone. 9-1-1 is only for people emergencies. But Mr. Carter, this is an animal emergency. My bird is hurt."

Officer Carter nodded toward his partner. "I'll go have a look. Shout if something comes up." Officer Martinez nodded and headed back to the car. Officer Carter followed Elena inside.

By now, Puzzle was sitting up, licking his paws. "Feathers

is over here on the couch," Elena said.

Officer Carter picked up the little lump of green feathers. "She's still breathing. Elena, your bird is probably in shock. That means she got too scared. If you wrap her up in a towel to keep her warm and talk to her, she should be OK."

"I'll hold her in my hand close to my chest," Elena decided. "I wish I had a packet."

Just then, Elena heard a voice outside by the street. "What's going on? Officer, is my baby OK?"

"Oops," Elena mumbled. "I forgot about . . ."

But the door crashed open before she could finish. "Elena, are you all right?"

"Sure, Mom. I'm fine." Elena tried to answer while her mother hugged her tight. "But Feathers is in shock."

"That makes two of us," Mom said, pushing Elena back at arm's length. "What are the police doing here?"

Elena tried to explain. "I was cleaning the cage like you told me, and Puzzle knocked it over, and Feathers flew, and I chased them, and the curtains fell on them, and, and . . ." Elena burst into tears and threw her arms around her mom's neck.

Cheep! The sound made Elena jump back. "Oh, Feathers! You're OK!" she said as looked into her hand.

Mom followed Officer Carter to the door. "Thank you so much. I'll make sure she understands."

Elena heard the locks click into place as she held Feathers up to her cheek. She knew what was coming next.

"Elena, we need to have a talk."

"Yes, Mom."

By the time she went to bed, Elena knew it by heart.

"Call 9-1-1 if you are hurt or in danger. Call 9-1-1 if you know another person is hurt or in danger. Otherwise, leave the police and the ambulances alone so they can help other people."

"This was all your fault," Elena whispered to Puzzle when he hopped up beside her pillow. "You deserved getting hit on the head."

Purrr-purrr. Puzzle closed his eyes and started his motor.

"Oh, well, I forgive you." Elena closed her eyes too.

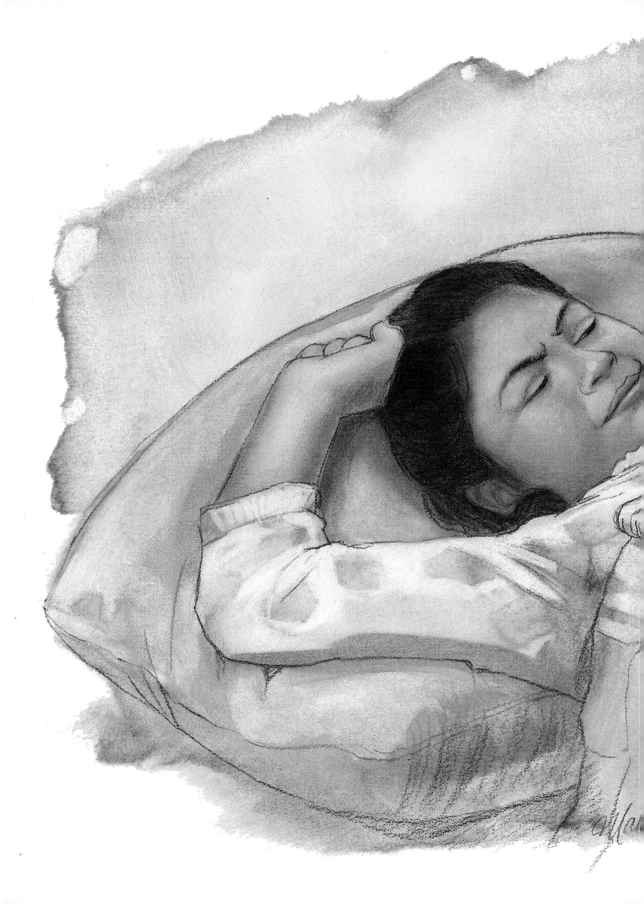

SMoKe!

One afternoon several weeks later, the key turned in the lock again. "Puzzle, I'm home." *Click, clunk, clack.* Elena locked the door behind her.

Meow, purrr-purrr. Puzzle came crying for attention. "Hello, boy," Elena said, stopping to scratch his belly. "Feathers, I'm home," she called.

Chir-reep! Feathers answered.

Elena fed her pets and herself and then sat down to watch TV. "Puzzle," she asked a few minutes later, "is something wrong?"

The cat was prowling around the room, sniffing at the windows and the door. *Meow?* He seemed to be asking a question.

Before long, Elena noticed it too. "What is that smell? Is something burning?" She looked around but didn't see any smoke. Then, from far away, she heard the sound of a siren.

"Do you think it's a firetruck?" she asked Puzzle. They

Latchkey kids; handling emergencies

both stared out the window and listened. "I think it's getting closer."

By the time the firetruck turned down Gulliver Street, Elena was pacing back and forth like Puzzle. "I wonder how close the fire is? I could go outside and look, but Mom told

me not to open the door for any reason."

The smell of smoke got stronger. As Elena watched, more cars and trucks with flashing lights on top turned down her street. When she saw smoke moving like a cloud across the street, she picked up the phone.

"Mom's phone is busy," she reported to Puzzle. Suddenly,

she felt scared. "What am I supposed to do? Should I call 9-1-1?"

Chir-reep! Cheep! Feathers had something to say.

"I know, Feathers. When I called 9-1-1, I got in trouble. But Mom said to call if I am in danger. Do you think I am?"

Neither the bird nor the cat had an answer for that. Another cloud of smoke drifting by her window helped Elena decide. She picked up the phone again and punched three buttons.

"Emergency Services," a woman's voice said.

Elena took a deep breath. "My name is Elena, and I'm not sure if this is an emergency. But there are firetrucks in front of my apartment. Is my building on fire? What should I do?"

"What's your address, Elena?"

"1458 Gulliver Street, Apartment 117."

"OK, let me find out. Stay with me." Elena could hear the woman asking questions and talking to other people. Then she came back on. "Elena, the fire is in the building next to yours. But you need to leave in case it spreads. Is an adult with you?"

"No, just my cat and my bird. And my mom told me not to open the door or leave the apartment until she gets home."

"Elena, your mother wants you to be safe. Can you see a police car from your window?"

Elena peeked out. "Yes."

"I want you to open your door, close it behind you, and walk straight to that police car. Tell an officer where you live and that you're alone. Someone will watch you until your mother can get there. Will you do that?"

"OK," Elena agreed. She set down the phone and walked toward the door.

Chir-reep!

"Feathers! I can't leave you." She ran and grabbed the bird's cage off its hook.

Meow?

"Puzzle! Come here." Elena set the cage down and gathered her cat up in her arms. "What am I going to do with you? If I try to carry you outside, you'll get down and run away. But I can't leave you here. I wish you could fit in my pocket like a bird."

That gave her an idea. A few seconds later, she was ready.

Smoke swirled in as Elena opened her door. Coughing, she set down the bird cage and pulled the door closed behind her. She could hear the crackling roar of the fire and the wailing of another firetruck, but she couldn't see through the smoke.

Elena's hand shook as she picked up the bird cage. *Don't be scared,* she told herself. *Everything will be OK if I can see enough to get away without running into something.* With one hand shielding her eyes, Elena headed down her steps.

Bonk! She ran right into something.

"Aaah!" Elena screamed. The bird cage slipped out of her hand and hit the step.

"Whoa!" A police officer grabbed the cage with one hand and Elena's arm with the other. "I've got you. Are you the girl who called 9-1-1?"

Elena just coughed and nodded.

"Good. I was just coming to make sure you got out." He smiled at the bird cage. "I see you got your pet out. There's no one else at your house, right?"

"Right."

"OK, let's go." As they crossed the street, Elena watched the flames shooting from the roof and windows of the building next to hers. The firefighters were spraying water on it from three different trucks.

The officer led the way out of the smoke and over to a

crowd of people standing behind a yellow ribbon. "Officer Carter," he shouted, "here's another one to keep an eye on."

Officer Carter came right over. He stared for a second and then remembered her. "Oh, it's you, our 9-1-1 caller."

Elena smiled. "I called again today, and they told me to come out here. So I did."

"Well, it looks like you did exactly the right thing this time. Come on over to the police car, and we'll try to get in touch with your mother."

After hearing that her mom was on her way home, Elena stood and watched the fire with the other people. Slowly, the water was beating the flames down.

Officer Carter stopped to report. "It looks as if your home is safe, Elena." He patted the bird cage. "I hope your other pet is OK."

"Oh, Feathers is fine," Elena answered, patting her pocket. "But Puzzle will be mad at me for a week. Won't you?" she added, kneeling down to scratch her cat's head.

Meow! Puzzle grumped from behind the bars of the bird cage.

Smoke!

Red Hawk Hero

Face off!"

Paul tapped his hockey stick on the ice as he stared at the puck in the referee's hand. He ignored the kid in the Blue Wings uniform.

Smack! Moving like a blur, Paul's stick connected before the puck even reached the ice. The Red Hawk on the back of his uniform seemed to fly as he took off down the ice.

"Go, go!" Coach Iverson shouted from the bench. Skating to his left, Paul watched the puck as his teammate Lars followed it to the corner. Lars's pass sent the puck flying between two Blue Wings players and out to Robert. Robert tapped it right out in front of Paul.

With a quick swing of his stick, Paul slapped the puck right under the goalie's glove and into the net.

"Goal!" the referee called.

"Yes!" Paul shouted as he made a quick turn. "Was that a great shot or what?" he called to Robert and Lars.

Dealing with pride; conceit

"We're up two to one!" Coach shouted. "Now do it again!" When the Red Hawks won, Paul chattered all the way to the dressing room. "I knew that last one was going in as soon as I slapped it," he explained to Lars. "I could just feel it."

"Just remember who passed the puck to you," Lars answered. "You weren't the only Red Hawk out there."

Paul felt confused. "I know. But I scored both goals. I won the game."

Robert shoved his way by. "Yeah, Paul was the hero. Just ask him," he said.

Paul shrugged and walked away. His mom and dad and Uncle Gerard were waiting outside. "Great game, son," Dad said.

Paul grinned. "Did you see that last goal? It was perfect."

Uncle Gerard nodded. "I saw it. It reminded me of a goal I scored in the championship game in high school. The puck was way out in front of everyone. Since I was the fastest skater, I got there first. The goalie didn't even have time to blink."

Later that week, Paul found his friends at Pederson's pond playing hockey. "Hey, guys, wait for me. I'll get my skates and come practice with you."

"Why bother?" Lars asked. "Someone as great as you doesn't need practice."

"That's why I am so good," Paul answered. "Because I practice a lot."

"Well, we don't need any heroes in this game," Robert called. "Maybe you should save your energy for those winning goals."

"Besides," Lars added, "we already know how good you are. You don't have to tell us again."

Paul just stood there. He wasn't sure what to say. Finally, he turned and walked slowly home. Without even taking off his coat, he lay down on the couch and closed his eyes.

"What have we here?" His mother came into the room. "A sick boy?"

Paul made a face. "I guess I'm just confused." He told her about Robert and Lars. "Why would they say that, Mother? Why don't they like me anymore?"

Mother sat down beside him on the couch. "Paul, I want to tell you about a boy who loved to play hockey like you do. And he was good—he could skate like the wind, and his shots were straight and true."

Paul smiled. "Like me."

Mother went on. "Whenever this boy made a goal, he jumped for joy. 'Did you see that?' he asked his friends. 'Wasn't that the best shot you ever saw?' When the puck was loose on the ice, he was always there first. 'I'm the fastest skater around,' he would say."

Suddenly, Paul wasn't smiling.

"Before long, he noticed that his friends weren't so friendly. They found excuses not to play hockey with him, and he often was left skating alone. 'They're just jealous,' he decided, 'because I'm better than they are.' So he went on to look for other friends who would appreciate his ability to play hockey."

"Mother, is this a story about me?"

Mother shook her head. "No, sadly it is not. It is a story of my brother, your Uncle Gerard."

"But, Mother, he is the best hockey player around!"

She nodded. "So he's told you many times, eh? But why do you think he spends almost every weekend with us?"

Paul shrugged. "He likes us?"

"I'm sure he does. But the truth is, he doesn't really have any other friends."

"He doesn't?" Paul was amazed. "But he can score a goal faster than you can blink."

"I know. He's been telling me that since he was your age. And everyone else." Mother looked straight into Paul's eyes. "Maybe you should think about that."

He thought about it the rest of the day.

The next afternoon at the game, Paul strapped on his skates without saying a word. "OK, guys," Coach Iverson said, "let's play like a team today."

Paul took his usual place at center ice. Before long, he was flying down the floor after the puck. *Shhush!* A quick turn, and the puck was on his stick. He passed across to Lars and headed for the goal.

Lars sent the puck up to Robert. Robert's pass led Paul right in front of the net. With a quick flick of the wrist, Paul launched the puck toward the top right corner. The goalie lunged for it, but he was too late.

"Goal!" the referee shouted.

"Great shot!" Coach yelled from the bench. Paul circled the goal, holding his stick over his head. Then he headed right over to Robert and Lars. *Shhush!* Ice shavings flew as he slid to a stop.

Robert looked away. Lars bit his lip. Then Paul said, "Great work, guys. That was a perfect pass, Robert." As he skated away, he couldn't resist turning back to look. Robert and Lars were both just standing there with their mouths hanging open.

"Let's go!" Coach shouted from the bench. Paul looked up as Robert skated past him into position.

Robert smiled. "Let's do it again!" he shouted.

HE HAD A DREAM

Deena stuck another french fry in her ketchup to let it soak. Usually, soaking french fries at Mandy's, her favorite place to eat out, made Deena happy. Today, she wasn't happy at all.

"I could have stayed home," she said for the tenth time.

"No, you couldn't," her sister Josie answered automatically. "Could she, Grandma?"

Their grandmother shook her head. "Now, Deena, you know we've been planning to go to the Martin Luther King Day parade for a long time."

"But Mom and Dad were supposed to go with us," Deena grumbled. "Besides, it's too cold."

"Deena, your mother and father didn't want to be out of town today. It just worked out that way. Besides, what would you do if you stayed at home?"

"I was going to play with Carrie," Deena answered.

"Well," Grandma said, standing up and collecting their

Dealing with ignorance; prejudice

trash onto the tray, "Carrie and Mark are going to the parade too."

"They are?" Josie liked that. "Isn't that great, Deena?"

Deena liked it too, but she still wanted to be mad, since she didn't want to go to the parade anyway.

"Come on," Grandma said, sliding her purse onto her arm and grabbing the three folded chairs. "It's time to catch the bus." The two girls followed her out the door into the cold air and to the bus stop. "Do you see the bus yet?" Grandma asked Deena.

Deena held onto the bus-stop post and leaned out toward

the street. Even through her glove, the post felt cold to her hand. "No. We'll probably freeze before it gets here."

"Nope," Josie called, leaning by her sister, "there it is! Grandma, can we sit in the very front seats and watch where we're going?"

Grandma handed each girl one of the chairs as the other riders crowded around. "If those seats are empty, we'll take them."

In a puff of exhaust, the bus pulled up, and the door *whooshed* open. Josie led the way to the front seats while Grandma paid. "How does the driver know where to take us?" Josie asked.

The driver heard her and laughed. "Are you folks going downtown to the parade?" Josie nodded. "Well, that's where I'm going too."

When the bus stopped again, the driver called, "All parade watchers, out here." The sisters clunked down the steps with their chairs and waited for Grandma to decide which way to go.

"This way," Grandma said. "I told Mark and Carrie's mother we'd be at the corner of Seventh and Main Street." Other people were settling in with chairs and blankets, too, as they found a place on the sidewalk.

Then they waited.

"How long do we have to wait?" Deena whined. She stomped her feet on the cold sidewalk. "Dr. Martin Luther King sure picked a bad time of the year to be born," she said. Her breath puffed out like smoke. "I don't know why we have to go to a parade or anything anyway."

"Hey, there're Mark and Carrie," Josie reported from the

street. "Over here!" she shouted, waving her arms. Before long, their friends had joined them.

After a minute, Mark asked, "Who is Martin Luther King, anyway? I like him because we get out of school for his birthday. But I don't know why we get out."

Deena rolled her eyes. "Dr. King was a great man. He did great things for black people. Everyone knows that. Right, Grandma?"

Grandma frowned. "The day's not really just about what Martin Luther King did," she said. "It's a day to celebrate equality. Let me explain. When I was your age, black people in this country didn't have the same rights as other people."

"What do you mean?" Josie asked.

"Well, for one thing, they couldn't eat in the same restaurants as white people."

"What?" Deena almost fell out of her chair. "You mean, you couldn't eat french fries at Mandy's?"

Grandma chuckled. "Well, that place wasn't here back in those days. But no, Deena, I couldn't eat in many restaurants like that one. Also, black people couldn't have the same kinds of jobs as white people. They couldn't even drink from the same drinking fountains."

Now, Deena got mad. "That's not right! They can't treat people like that!"

Grandma nodded. "But they did. In those days, black people had to ride at the back of buses, not in the front as we did this morning. And black children like you had to go to different schools. Separating people in that way is called segregation."

Carrie grabbed Deena's hand. "You mean we couldn't be in the same class? I wouldn't like that at all."

"Why?" Mark asked. "Why were people so mean and stupid?"

Grandma frowned. "Do you know what the word *ignorant* means?"

Josie knew. "It means not knowing something."

"Most Americans had been told that black people just weren't as important or special as whites," Grandma said. "They weren't being mean or stupid. They were just ignorant."

Carrie's dad spoke up. "Not everyone thought that way, though. Many people, both black and white, spoke up against segregation. Especially Dr. King."

"So Dr. King made them change the laws?" Mark asked.

"Not really," Grandma said. "Other people protested first. But Dr. King began speaking against the laws in public. He made people who were ignorant stop and think about how black people were treated. And when they did, most decided that he was right."

"He led marches with thousands of people," Carrie's mom added, "to demand that black people be given the same rights as white people."

"Dr. King had a dream," Grandma said. "He dreamed that one day all children of every color would be equally loved and that all people would live together in peace."

"But someone shot him," Josie said sadly.

Grandma nodded. "Yes. Someone who hated the changes he was demanding killed him. But his dream lives on, and today, black people, brown people, white people, all people are treated the same by the laws of America and by the good people who live here."

"I'm glad for that," Carrie said, smiling at Deena.

"Me too," Deena said. Then she hugged her grandmother. "Sorry I was so grumpy. I guess I was ignorant too. But not anymore!"

From up the street, they heard the sound of trumpets. "Here comes the first marching band!" Mark shouted.

For some reason, Deena wasn't so cold anymore.

"Tattletale"

17

Mom! Megan's playing with her food!"

Megan made a face across the table at her sister, Melissa. "Tattletale!" she hissed as she pulled her spoon out of a piece of toast. Their big sister, Monica, rolled her eyes.

"Megan, stop playing and finish eating," Mom said as she walked into the room. "If we waste all our time this morning, we won't be able to go swimming this afternoon. Everyone's room has to be clean before we swim," she added.

The thing I like most about living next to a lake is getting to swim every day, Melissa said to herself. She cleaned her room quickly and put on her swimsuit. *If Megan and Monica aren't cleaning their rooms, I won't get to swim. I'd better go see.*

Before long, Melissa was shouting,

Being a tattletale

"Mom, Megan isn't cleaning her room. She's watching TV."

"Megan," Mom called back, "turn the TV off. You won't swim until that room is clean."

Melissa stuck her head in Monica's room. It was clean. But Monica was trying on one of Mom's new T-shirts. Melissa ran to the kitchen. "Mom, Monica is wearing your new blue shirt," she announced.

Mom rolled her eyes and headed for Monica's room. Before long, she was back. "Lissa, come here." Melissa sat down, her swimming towel in her lap. Mom patted her leg. "Lissa, why do you tell on your sisters?"

Melissa stared at her hands.

"Do you just need attention? Or are you trying to make Megan and Monica look bad?"

Melissa looked up. "My room is clean."

Mom tilted her head. "Lissa, I like what you did in your room more than I like what Megan did. I like the fact that you're wearing your own clothes more than I like what Monica did. But I love them just the same as I do you."

Melissa blinked twice.

"And I don't like it when you tattle. Yes, Megan should have been cleaning her room, and Monica isn't supposed to wear my shirt. But you're not the police for your sisters. That's my job."

Melissa swallowed. "What should I do when I see them doing something wrong?"

Mom thought for a second. "If Megan is trying to write her name in the dirt with my screwdriver, you might remind her that she's not supposed to play with my tools. But you don't need to tell me."

Melissa nodded. "It's between you and her."

"Right. Now, if she's trying to scratch her name on the car with my screwdriver, you should tell her to stop. And if she doesn't, you should tell me."

"If she's tearing something up, then tell you," Melissa repeated.

Mom raised her finger. "And if someone is doing something dangerous, then telling is always the right thing to do. Lissa, I want to help you remember this. So for the rest of the day, if you tattle on Megan or Monica for anything that's not dangerous or destructive, you'll get the same punishment they do. Do you understand?"

Melissa's eyes got big, but she nodded. For the rest of the

morning, she tried not to talk at all. *That way,* she thought, *I won't forget and tattle about something.*

She didn't say anything when Megan skipped brushing her teeth after lunch. She kept her mouth closed when Monica took a dessert cookie to her room.

"OK, girls, I guess it's time for a swim," Mom finally said. She led them to the back porch and put sunscreen lotion on Megan and Melissa. "Don't forget your lotion too," she called as Monica headed to the beach. "Megan, here's your life jacket."

"Wait, I have to go to the bathroom first," Megan insisted.

I'm glad I don't have to wear a life jacket this year, Melissa said to herself as she waited. She was a good swimmer now, but Megan was still learning.

Just as Megan got back, the phone rang. "You go ahead," Mom called. "I'll be there in a few minutes."

At the beach, Melissa dropped her towel by Monica. "Hey, Mom said to put on sunscreen," Melissa reminded her.

"I don't want to," Monica replied. "I want a tan."

Melissa went back into the house. "Mom?" she said, tugging at her mother's sleeve as she talked. "Mom, Monica . . ."

Mom looked at her and raised one eyebrow. Suddenly, Melissa froze. *Oops! I forgot. No tattling.* She turned and headed for the lake without saying another word.

She almost tripped over something orange. It was Megan's life jacket. "Hey, you're supposed to keep this on all the time," she said to her sister.

Megan was sitting in the shallow water. "It's too hot. Besides, I can swim a little."

Melissa had taken two steps toward the house and opened her mouth to shout "Mom!" before she remembered. *I can't*

tattle. When Mom sees Megan down here without that jacket, she won't let her swim for a week! I don't want to get the same punishment. I'm keeping my mouth shut.

"Tattletale"

As the minutes went by without Mom showing up, Megan splashed farther out into the water. Melissa got more and more worried. "Come on, Megan, put on your life jacket. You know you have to have it on."

"I don't need it," Megan said with a sniff. "And don't be a tattletale."

Melissa closed her mouth, but inside she was bubbling. *I wish Mom would hurry and come out here. Should I tell on Megan? I don't want to get in trouble, but should I?*

Finally, she hopped up and ran to the house. Her mom was still on the phone. "Yes, that's what he said. A fish and bait shop. Like we need another one of those!"

Melissa tugged at her sleeve. "Mom. Mom!"

Mom put her hand over the phone. "What is it, Lissa? Not tattling again, I hope."

Melissa took a deep breath, then nodded. "Megan took her life jacket off."

"What?" Mom hissed. "Go over to that window and shout for her to come here."

Melissa ran to the window and pushed back the curtains. "Megan, Mom says come here! Megan?" She ran back to her mother. "Mom, I don't see her at all!"

Mom's eyes got big. She dropped the phone and ran. Melissa was right behind her. As they ran, Melissa saw Megan's head pop to the surface of the water, then disappear.

A short time later, Mom sat holding a very wet and very frightened Megan. "I slipped under the water," Megan explained tearfully. "Then I stood up, but I couldn't reach the top."

"I'm sorry I wasn't watching better," Monica said, patting her little sister's arm.

"Melissa was," Mom said. "She knew it was dangerous."

Megan smiled a tiny smile. "I'm glad you were a tattletale this time, Lissa."

Melissa smiled too. "I'm glad you're OK."

Mom patted Monica's back. "I'm glad everyone's OK."

Monica jerked away. "Ow, not so hard. I have a sunburn."

Melissa opened her mouth. Then she closed it without saying a word.

Secret Missions

18

The sleeve of Sara's coat tickled Ben's nose. He leaned back against the wall of the closet and tried not to sneeze.

Sara had the phone. Her voice came in through the small open slit of the closet door. "Jenna told me that Eric said that Bobby likes me. Is she telling the truth?"

Ben whipped out his tiny flashlight and his little blue notebook. Holding the flashlight between his teeth, he pulled out his pencil and wrote *Bobby likes Sara.*

"Super Spy McFly strikes again," he whispered with a grin. He pushed the door open another inch and peered out at his sister.

"Well, don't tell anyone," Sara said. "It has to be a secret." She turned toward the window, so Ben pushed the door open and crawled out of the room.

"Another secret mission completed," he said as he stood up and walked down the hall. His other sister, Rachel, stepped

Privacy; respect

out of the bathroom.

"What secret mission?" she asked. "What are you up to now, Ben?"

"Nothing," Ben said, raising his hands. "I don't know anything." He backed away until she disappeared into her room. Then he headed downstairs.

His brother Josh was halfway out the back door. "Mom, I'm going over to Antonio's. I'll be back by suppertime."

Ben heard his mother answer "OK" and knew the coast was clear. *Now, Super Spy McFly will dig up new secrets about the enemy,* he said to himself. Josh's bedroom door was closed, but Ben didn't even slow down. He was inside in a flash.

"First target—desk drawer," Ben said. He pawed through the papers there. "Math homework, science homework—ah, ha! Social-studies test. And Josh got a 'D.' I think Mom might like to know that." He wrote a quick note in his blue notebook

and kept looking. "Let's try the school books," Ben muttered next. He opened Josh's folders and flipped through the pages. Some scribbling caught his eye.

"Josh—The day after school is out is the first day it's open. Whoever's there first has the best chance—Lindsay"

"Lindsay—Let's not tell anyone else about it—Josh"

Ben scribbled in his notebook again. Then a voice in the hallway grabbed him.

"Yeah, I forgot my basketball." It was Josh!

Ben dove for the floor and rolled under the bed as the door opened. Josh's tennis shoes were only inches from his head.

"Where is that ball?" Josh said out loud. Then he snapped his fingers. "Under the bed."

Ben's eyes were almost as big as the basketball beside his head. He pushed it toward the edge and ducked away as Josh's hands came into view.

"Here we go." The ball disappeared, and Josh went out the door. Ben actually started breathing again.

"Super Spy McFly outsmarts the enemy agent and escapes," he said as he crawled out. "As fast as he can!"

At supper that evening, Ben passed a smirk on to Sara along with the corn. "So, how is Bobby today?" he asked.

Sara turned as red as the tomatoes. "How would I know? I haven't seen him."

Rachel leaned over and whispered in her ear. Then she leaned forward and glared at Ben.

"Why are you asking about Bobby?" Rachel demanded.

Ben just smiled smugly. "Super Spy McFly knows everything," he said as he crunched a carrot.

"Where did you get this McFly name?" Mom asked. "It sounds strange."

Ben rolled his eyes. "It's a code name, Mom. All the spies have them."

Josh snorted and reached into his pocket. "Tell me this, Spy Fly. Why did I find this in my room?" He tossed a little blue notebook onto the table.

Ben's hand flew to his pocket. *I must have dropped it when I crawled under the bed!* He reached out to grab it.

"Not so fast." Josh pinned Ben's hand to the table. "What

was it doing in my room?"

Dad stepped in. "Josh, let go of your brother. Ben, is that your notebook?"

Ben grabbed it before he answered. "Yes. You didn't read it, did you?" he asked Josh.

"No. I don't snoop into other people's things," Josh answered as he stabbed at his mashed potatoes. "What were you doing in my room?"

Ben saw that his parents were waiting for an answer too. "I, uh, was looking for the basketball."

"Stay out of my room unless you ask first," Josh demanded.

"OK, I think that's settled," Mom said. "Now let's get back to eating."

"But, Mom," Sara whined, "Ben's always sneaking around with this spy stuff. He's always trying to find out our secrets."

Ben laughed. "That's what Super Spy McFly does."

"Well, I think it's annoying," Rachel added.

"I think the solution is for everyone to try and get along," Mom said.

Josh stared across the table. "I think the solution is a big flyswatter."

Mom set her fork down. "If you can't get along at this table, I'm not taking any of you to the health-club swimming pool. You can wait until the park pool opens after school's out."

"I'm getting along, I'm getting along," Sara said quickly. "We're still going tomorrow night, aren't we?"

"Not until Thursday," Ben said. Then it hit him. "Oops." He sank down in his chair.

Sara stared at him. "How do you know?"

Dad stared too. "I had the same question, Ben. I just

changed my plans at work today. And I only talked to Mom
about it on the phone this afternoon. So, you want to explain
this?"

Mom jumped in before he had the chance. "Benjamin! You
were listening in on the other phone, weren't you?"

Rachel chimed in. "I told you, Mom."

"You must have listened to my phone call this afternoon
too!" Sara said angrily. "You little rat!"

"You mean 'fly,' " Josh added.

Dad raised his hand. "Ben?"

"Well, I picked the phone up at the same time Mom did,
and since it was you, I was going to say Hi. But I didn't." Ben
tried a fake smile, but it didn't help.

Dad wasn't smiling. "You and I will have a little talk in your
room after supper, son."

"OK." Ben ate slowly, but his mind was racing. *Super Spy
McFly prepares to be tortured. How will he escape this time?*

The Case of the Mysterious Place

Super Spy McFly paces back and forth in his cell. Can he escape before the torturer arrives? Ben grabbed his notebook and headed for the window.

"Ben?" Dad's voice at the door ended those thoughts. He came in. "Let's talk. Come and sit by me," he said, patting the spot beside him on the bed. He reached for the blue notebook. "Can I see that?"

Ben handed it over slowly. "You don't have to read it, do you?"

"Why shouldn't I?"

Ben thought for a second. "Well, because it's mine. It's my Super Spy McFly notebook. If you read it, you might laugh. It's just a game I play, Dad."

Dad flipped the pages between his fingers. "Ben, what you're telling me is that this belongs to you and it's private."

"Right," Ben agreed. He reached for the notebook, but Dad held on to it.

Privacy; respect

"Tell me, Ben, why is it OK for you to have something private but not anyone else?"

Ben shrugged. "Everyone else can have . . ." he stopped before he finished the sentence. Even he could see the problem with that. "I'm not trying to hurt anyone. It's just a game."

Dad patted his arm. "Ben, there are two words you need to understand—*privacy* and *respect*. Giving someone his or her privacy means letting that person have a right to keep some things personal."

Ben agreed. "Like my notebook."

Dad nodded. "Yes, but it's more than that. People need privacy when they change clothes or take a bath. They also need privacy sometimes when they talk. Everyone should have a right to talk without someone secretly listening to their private conversations."

Ben hung his head. "Sorry about that."

"Respect means that you care enough about people to treat them with kindness. You give them their rights, including the right to privacy. If playing your spy game the way you do means invading their privacy, then you should choose not to play it that way."

Ben nodded.

Dad went on. "You should have respect for all people, Ben. And part of that respect means giving them their privacy."

The next day, Super Spy McFly did much better. He hid from people as they passed by his yard and imagined that they were enemy agents. "The blue car drove by again today," he muttered as he wrote *blue car* in his notebook. "It could be part of a plot to take over the country."

But something was tickling the back of Ben's mind. He flipped back through his notebook pages. *Ah, ha!* he said to himself. *It's from what was written in Josh's science folder.*

He read it out loud. "Lindsay says, 'The day after school is out is the first day it's open. Whoever's there first has the best chance.' And Josh says, 'Let's not tell anyone else about it.' Tomorrow is the last day of school. I wonder what they were talking about?"

Later that afternoon, Ben walked through the living room up to the kitchen door but stopped when he heard voices inside. "The first ten people waiting in line get in free," Rachel said.

"School will be out," Sara added. "We won't even have to bother Mom and Dad. We'll walk over there."

Ah, ha! Sara and Rachel know about it too. Super Spy McFly is on the case! The Case of the Mysterious Place!

Ben backed away into the living room. "I've got to get more information," he muttered. And there, right on the table, were Sara's school books.

Well, he thought, *Sara left them right out here in the living room. If she wants her school books and folders to be private, she should keep them in her room.*

He kept one eye on the kitchen door while he flipped through Sara's papers. Suddenly, her handwriting on the back of a book report grabbed his attention.

"Let's not even tell him about it. That'll teach him a thing or two—the little rat!"

"What are they trying to keep from me?" Ben scratched his head. "I've got to find out more."

A few minutes later, Ben was huddled on the floor of his sisters' closet. He didn't have long to wait. He heard both girls talking as they entered the room.

"Are you going to Cindy's before supper?" Rachel asked.

"I want to," Sara answered. "But Mom says our room has to be clean before I can go anywhere."

"Well, I'm going to Angela's, so let's get this done. I'll make the beds if you'll put the clothes away."

Ben could hear the shuffling, grunting sounds of them working. Then he heard something far worse.

"Where should I put all this?" Sara asked.

"Just throw it in the closet," Rachel answered.

Ben was already thinking of ways to apologize when the closet door flew open. Before he could say a word, he was covered with clothes.

"Unless Mom looks in the closet," Sara said, "she'll think I carried all our dirty clothes down to the laundry room.

Ben waited until he heard the girls leave before he pushed

clothes off his head and took a deep breath. Then he wished he hadn't. "Phew! I know spies have to go to dangerous places, but this is too much."

His next big chance didn't come until the next night. Since school was over, he got to stay out until after dark. "Super Spy McFly is on the case," he whispered as he crawled behind the bush under his brother's window. The window was open to the cool evening breeze. Josh had the phone in his room and was talking to someone.

"So are you ready for tomorrow? . . . Oh, is he a lifeguard?"

Great, Ben thought, *this is what I wanted to find out. Nothing can go wrong now.*

But something did. Someone grabbed his pants leg.

First in Line

Wedged behind the bush, Ben couldn't even turn around to see who he was in trouble with. "I can explain," he started to whisper.

"*Meow?*"

It was the neighbor's cat.

"Go away," Ben hissed. The cat purred and meowed even louder. When Ben tried to shove it away, it jumped up on the windowsill.

"Meow!"

Ben tried to grab one of its legs. "Come back, nice kitty. Come down from there."

He heard Josh's voice from inside. "Hold on a second. Get away from my window! How many times do I have to tell you to leave me alone?"

"I-I'm sorry," Ben started to say. Suddenly, the cat hissed as it jumped away. Water poured down on Ben's head.

"Sorry," Josh said inside. "This cat keeps bugging me. I

Privacy; respect

just threw a glass of water at it. . . . No, it's gone now. So, let's go early before anyone else gets there."

Ben backed out and walked to his room dripping. After a few swipes with a towel, he grabbed a clean shirt and sat on his bed.

A good spy looks at his clues and figures out the answer, he told himself as he pulled out his notebook. *It happens the first day after school's out. The first ten people in line get in free. Sara and Rachel and Josh know about it. It happens somewhere close enough for them to walk to. And they're trying to leave me out.*

Then he remembered what Josh had said. *Lifeguard!* He snapped his fingers. *That's it! The park pool must be opening tomorrow, and the first ten people there get in free. So that's what they were trying to trick me out of. Ha! No one fools Super Spy McFly!*

He dug out his swimsuit. *Josh said something about going early to get there before anyone else does. So I'd better wake up extra early.*

When Ben's alarm went off, it was just barely light outside. "I'll be there first for sure," he said as he pulled on his shoes and grabbed a towel. Without making a sound, he slipped out the kitchen door and down the street to the park.

"Just as I thought," he said beside the locked gate around the silent pool, "no one is here yet. I can't wait to see the look on Sara's and Rachel's faces when they see me. I'll be first in line!"

Ben shivered a little as a slight drizzle began to fall. "I can't wait to see their faces," he repeated. After several long minutes, a park truck drove up. "Finally, they're here to open the pool," he said.

"Good morning," the man from the truck called. "What brings you out here so early?"

"I'm waiting for the pool to open," Ben said. "I wanted to be first in line."

The man looked surprised. "Well, you're certainly first. But you have kind of a long wait. The pool doesn't open until next week."

"What?" Ben almost dropped his towel. "Are you sure?" The man pointed to a sign on the fence, then walked away. Ben read the sign. *He's right. I must be a super-dumb spy.* He walked slowly toward home. *I feel really stupid.*

In a few minutes, he felt something else. It started pouring down rain.

Ben didn't think about it anymore. He put the towel over his head and ran home. Then he jerked the kitchen door open and jumped in. When he looked out from under the towel, the whole family was staring at him.

Josh stopped chewing his muffin. "Kind of early for a swim, isn't it?"

Ben blinked. "It's your fault. Didn't you say the pool was going to open the day after school—and that you were going there early?"

Josh lifted one eyebrow. "Lindsay and I are going to apply to work as lifeguards for the summer. And like I told her on the phone, we're going early this afternoon to do that."

Ben rushed on. "Rachel, you said it too. You said that the first ten people in line today would get in free."

"Boy, are you mixed up," Rachel answered over her toast. "I said the first ten people in line at the museum next week get in free. And I didn't say it to you."

Ben turned to Sara. "You were the one trying to keep it

from me. I read it on your book report. You said it would
teach me a lesson."

Sara sipped her hot chocolate. "I was talking about Bobby.
And I wasn't writing it for you to read."

Ben just stood there and dripped. "Well, son," Mom finally said, "I hope this teaches you a lesson. Your father thought you understood when he talked to you about privacy and respect."

Ben sagged and shivered. "I'm sorry. I guess I forgot. I don't think I'll forget anymore."

Before the day was over, Ben rushed through the living room with his notebook and magnifying glass. "Whoa," Mom said, "I thought you were through with this spy stuff."

Ben handed her a card. "I had to give up on people," he said. "They're too much trouble."

The card said,

Super Spy McFly

Does your cat need tracking?
Does your dog need following?
Call in a professional.
Call Super Spy McFly.
Always on duty (until school starts).

HANNAH'S TESTS

21

Hannah!"

Hannah ignored the whisper from behind her and looked at the next question on her test.

7. When the molecules of water slow down, it becomes a solid. This solid is known as

    a. mercury.

    b. hydrogen.

    c. ice.

Hannah chewed her eraser for a second, then circled c. Before she could answer the next one, a pencil hit her in the back. She turned to glare at Nicholas. "What?"

"What's the answer to number 7?" he whispered.

Hannah just rolled her eyes and turned back to her own test. *If Nicholas thinks I'm going to help him cheat, he's crazy,* she thought. As she looked at the next questions, Hannah felt

Dealing with cheating; friends

Hannah's Tests

141

pretty good. She had studied hard for this test, and she was ready.

Just as she turned to the last page, someone bumped her arm. It was E.J., on her way to the front to hand in her test. When E.J. turned to head back to her desk, Hannah moved her mouth without making any sound. "Wow! You finished first."

E.J. smiled. "N.P.," she mouthed back.

No problem, Hannah figured. Ever since she had known E.J., she'd had to figure out E.J.'s messages. E.J. loved to use just the first letters of words, instead of saying the phrase itself.

"It's because of my name," E.J. explained once. "If I can use initials for my name, I can use them for anything."

"Why not just use your real name?" Hannah had asked.

E.J. snorted. "If you had a name like Elyssa Jane, would you use it? I.D.T.S."

I don't think so, Hannah had finally figured out. By now, she was used to her friend's funny way of talking. The two of them usually competed to see who could get the best scores. But since they studied together, they usually got about the same grades.

Hannah already knew what she wanted to be when she grew up. "I'm going to be a people doctor," she had told E.J. She had to say it that way because E.J. wanted to be a doctor too—an animal doctor.

"Maybe we can share the same office," E.J. had said. "I'll be a veterinarian and treat the sick animals, and you can treat their sick owners."

"You must have really studied for that test," Hannah said to E.J. as they waited in line at the cafeteria for lunch. "Unless you just guessed at every question," she added with a laugh.

"No, I got them all right," E.J. replied. "The test wasn't that hard."

"I guess Nicholas thought it was," Hannah said. "He tried to get me to tell him one of the answers. Like I would really cheat for him. I'm going to tell Ms. Cho."

E.J. turned to get her tray. "You didn't answer him, did you?"

"No."

"Then he didn't really cheat, did he? Besides, it's not your job to worry about Nicholas. Let Ms. Cho catch him if he's cheating. I.H.P."

It's her problem, Hannah thought. "I guess you're right," she agreed. "But it still makes me mad. Oh, good," she added when she saw the food. "Tacos again."

"Did you finish your math?" E.J. asked after they returned their trays. "I still have five problems to go, so I'm going back to the class-room early to work on them."

Hannah's math was finished, but she went with E.J. "What's that?" she asked when E.J. pulled out a thin green-and-silver box.

· "It's my new calcula-tor," E.J. answered. "It's a H.B.P. from my dad."

Happy-birthday present, Hannah figured. "Can I try it?" E.J. handed it over, and Hannah opened the top and pushed the On button. "This is great," she said. "It has a little keyboard with all the letters like a little computer."

E.J. nodded. "It's a calculator and a diary. I can write notes to myself, keep a list of all my homework, or anything. See, push this one."

Hannah pushed the button. "Remind Mom to get more shampoo. Tell Dad the dog barfed in the garage," she read out loud. "E.J., this is great. Well, not the part about the dog, but everything else. Do you use it for a diary?"

"You mean, do I write personal things in there that I don't want anyone else to see?" E.J. asked. "Yes, I do. But it's in the secret part. No one can read it without my password."

"Wow, a secret password! What is it?"

"If I told you, it wouldn't be secret," E.J. said. "Now, be quiet so I can do this math."

Hannah played with the diary while E.J. worked. Other kids were coming in when E.J. said, "OK, I need my calculator."

"Are you sure?" Hannah asked.

"Yes!" E.J. insisted. "Ms. Cho said we could check our work with a calculator. It's not cheating."

"I know," Hannah said. "I just wanted to show it off to someone."

"Give me that," E.J. demanded, taking it from her friend. "And G.A."

I'm going away, Hannah said to herself as she headed for her desk. *I wish I had a calculator like that one.*

A few weeks later, Hannah and E.J. waited at the curb of the crosswalk after school. "Do you want to come over this afternoon?" Hannah asked. "We could do our social studies."

E.J. shook her head. "I'm supposed to baby-sit my little brother until Mom

gets home. Then we're all supposed to go to the mall. You want to go with us?"

Hannah's head shook as the crossing guard motioned for them to cross. "I have chores to do. And homework. When are you going to study? You know the test is tomorrow."

"I'll be ready," E.J. said. "S.Y.L."

"See you later," Hannah repeated.

The next morning, E.J. looked tired. "I guess I stayed up too late," she answered Hannah's question.

"Studying?" Hannah asked.

E.J. looked puzzled for a second. "Oh, you mean the social studies test. Yeah, I studied a little."

When Ms. Cho handed out the tests, Hannah got busy. Before long, she was chewing on her eraser. She read the question over again.

14. Land surrounded by water on three sides is called
a. an island.
b. a peninsula.
c. a valley.

Hannah circled *b* and went on to the next one. As she did, E.J. brushed by. *How can she be finished already?* Hannah wondered. *She must have guessed at a lot of them.* She smiled at E.J. as she passed by on her way back.

Hannah watched E.J. sit down, click her calculator closed, and put it in her backpack. As she turned back, Hannah shook her head. *I wish I could finish tests that quickly.* She had already answered the next question, when another thought hit her.

Why did E.J. have her calculator out for social studies?

CHEATER!

"Hannah!"

Hannah rolled her eyes at the whisper from behind her, but she turned around anyway. "What, Nicholas?"

"What did you get on your social studies test?"

"I don't know. Ms. Cho hasn't handed mine back yet." Hannah watched as her teacher handed tests back several rows away.

"I got 82 percent!" Nicholas said proudly. Then he pretended to be examining his test as Ms. Cho approached.

"Hannah, here's yours," Ms. Cho said as she set the test upside down on Hannah's desk. "You did very well."

Hannah flipped it over and stared at the score—94 percent! She held it up so Nicholas could see. "Better luck next time," she hissed.

"I could get a 94 percent if I studied all the time like you do," Nicholas grumbled.

Dealing with cheating; friends

"I doubt it," Hannah teased. But Nicholas was right about one thing—she liked to get good grades, so she did study a lot. Past Nicholas, she saw E.J. look at her test, then stuff it into her backpack.

Oh, dear. E.J. probably got a bad grade. Hannah knew she usually got better grades than her friend. Usually, they studied together. *I wonder if she studied at all.*

At lunch, she asked, "How did you do on the test, E.J.?"

E.J. shrugged. "I did fine. What are you doing after school? Want to go roller-skating? Mom said she would take us."

"Sure. I'll have to call my mom and ask her, though."

After lunch, they stopped at a pay phone in the school lobby. "Rats," Hannah said, patting her pockets. "I don't have a quarter."

"I think I have one," E.J. said. She set her backpack down and started pulling things out. "Here, hold this." She handed her calculator/diary to Hannah.

Hannah watched as the books and papers came out. On top of the pile she saw the social studies test. She looked once, then looked again. *E.J. got a 96 percent! How did she do that? And why didn't she tell me?*

"Here it is," E.J. said, holding up a shiny quarter. Then she saw Hannah staring at her. "What?"

"You got a 96 percent on your test," Hannah said, pointing at the paper.

E.J.'s face got a little red. "So? I did fine, like I said. W.T.P.?"

What's the problem? Hannah

was confused. "You didn't tell me! And you always brag when you get a better grade than I do. Besides, you said you didn't have time to study that night."

E.J.'s face got really red. "I—I guess I just got lucky. Come on. Are you going to call your mother or what?"

Before many more days had gone by, it was time for another science test. "Your test is tomorrow," Ms. Cho announced. "You may work in pairs and study for the rest of the period."

Hannah dragged her desk back beside E.J.'s. "Let's make a list of all the words we need to know," she suggested. "Then we'll write down the definitions and match them."

"OK," E.J. agreed, reaching for her backpack. She pulled out her calculator/diary and pushed the On button.

"This isn't math," Hannah reminded her.

"I know. I'm going to write our

list in my diary. Then I can study from it later. G.I., right?"

"Yeah, I guess it is a good idea," Hannah agreed. "Now, let's get started."

The next day, Hannah's pencil eraser was between her teeth again.

23. The level of rock beneath the crust of the earth is
 called the
 a. mantle.
 b. middle.
 c. core.

Hannah circled *a* and sighed. *This test is harder than I thought. I wonder how E.J.'s doing?* She turned and looked just as E.J. reached up and pushed a button on her calculator/diary. E.J. stared at it for a second, then marked another answer on her test.

Suddenly, Hannah put two and two together. *So that's it! E.J. is cheating on her tests. She's looking at the answers she wrote in her diary when we were studying.*

Hannah was so mad she bit the eraser right off her pencil.

She was still mad when E.J. got in line behind her in the cafeteria. "So what kind of slop are they trying to feed us today?" E.J. asked.

Hannah carefully said nothing.

E.J. tried again. "Hello, anyone home? Earth to Hannah— are you H.O.H.?"

Hannah whirled around. "I am not hard of hearing. I am mad at you. I don't think I wish to speak to you right now."

E.J. didn't say anything else, but she followed Hannah to a table in the corner. "What is it?" she asked as she slammed

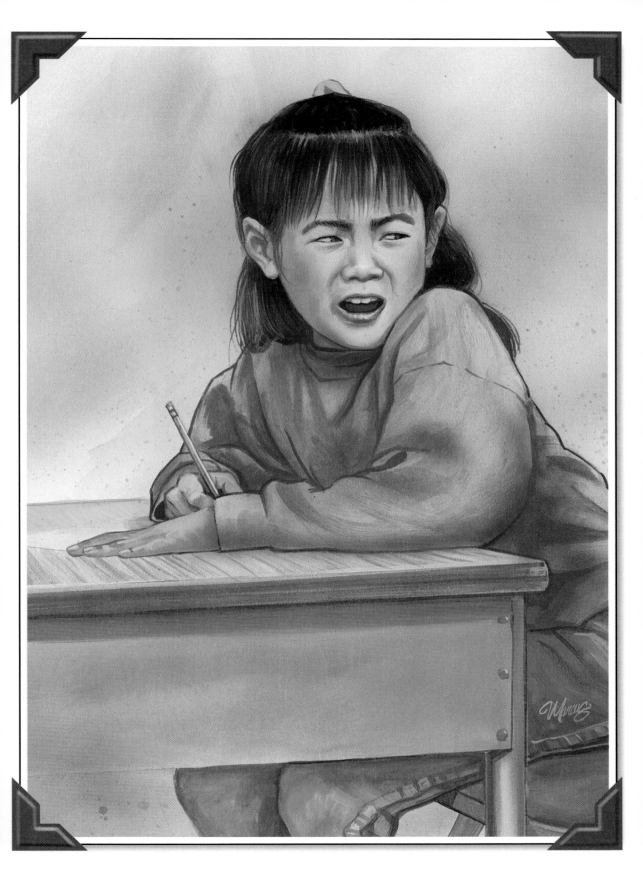

down her tray. "I didn't do anything to you."

Hannah stared at her. "You cheated on our science test this morning. And you've been cheating for weeks." She waved her spoon when E.J. started to speak. "I saw you looking up the answers in your diary. Why are you cheating?"

E.J.'s mouth opened, then closed. When it opened again, she said, "Why not? It's easier than studying."

"E.J.! Cheating is wrong!"

"It's not wrong unless you get caught," E.J. insisted. "Lots of kids cheat in school. Besides, why do you care? You get the same grades whether I cheat or not."

"It's still wrong," Hannah said. "You're lying to Ms. Cho about what you've learned."

E.J. dropped her fork. "And I guess you're going to have to do the right thing and tell on me. Well, I have a message for you—if you want to be my friend, M.Y.O.B.!"

A Friend's Business

Hannah."

The voice wasn't a whisper, but Hannah didn't hear it anyway. She was busy thinking. In her mind, she kept hearing E.J.'s voice. "If you want to be my friend, mind your own business!"

Maybe she's right. Maybe I should just forget about it. Then everything will go back to being the same as before. But somehow, she knew it wouldn't happen.

"Hannah."

Hannah still didn't respond. She kept pushing her green peas around on her plate.

"Hannah!" Finally, she looked up. It was her mother. "Hannah, I think those peas are dead now.

Dealing with cheating; friends

You can eat them."

Hannah didn't even laugh. "Mom, what would you do if you didn't know what to do?"

Mom thought for a second. "I don't know. I guess I'd tell my mother about the problem and see if she could help."

Now it was Hannah's turn to think. Finally, she said, "I know this person at school—I'm not saying who," she said pointedly, "who's cheating on her tests."

Mom nodded. "And this bothers you?"

"Mom, it's wrong!"

"Why?"

"Mom! You know why. It's dishonest. It's like lying to the teacher. And to your parents, because the grades you bring home aren't really ones you've earned."

"Hannah, I understand why you don't cheat. Why does it matter to you whether someone else does?"

Hannah had to think about that. "Well, it's not fair to everyone else in the class who studies for their grades."

"So why don't you just tell your teacher and let her deal with it? You could even write a note to Ms. Cho about it and not sign your name."

"It wouldn't work." Hannah sighed. "The person would know who told. And if I tell, we won't be friends anymore."

After another minute of watching Hannah push peas, Mom said, "Are you going to keep being friends if you don't tell?"

Hannah thought. "We never study together anymore. And comparing grades will just make me mad. Besides," she added quietly, "if she doesn't mind lying to everyone else, maybe she's lying to me about things too."

"Hannah, I can't tell you what to do. But your friendship with E.J. is going to change, whether you tell or not. And think about one more thing—who is E.J. really cheating?"

It took a second, but Hannah caught it. "Mom, I never said I was talking about E.J."

Mom got up. "Right. Like you're going to be this upset about someone else. She's your friend, Hannah. And friendship is worth trying to save."

Hannah left early the next morning. She waited at the crossing until E.J. showed up. "Can I talk to you?" she asked.

E.J. looked suspicious. "I guess." They walked to a bench in front of the school and sat down.

Hannah took a deep breath. "You said if I wanted us to keep being friends, I should mind my own business. And I've decided to do that—at least I'm not telling Ms. Cho."

E.J. smiled.

"But I have something to tell you. If you're going to keep cheating, I don't think we can keep being friends."

E.J.'s eyes got big. Hannah went on before E.J. could say anything.

"Think about it. We wouldn't be studying together anymore. We couldn't compete for the best grades or anything. If you showed me your grades, it would just make me mad."

E.J. was silent.

"Besides, if you don't mind lying to Ms. Cho or to your parents about the grades you get, how do I know you won't be lying to me too?"

"But I wouldn't," E.J. protested.

"Let me finish," Hannah demanded. She wanted to be done before any tears started. "Who do you think you're cheating, anyway? Ms. Cho? You might be hurting her feelings, but the only person you're cheating is you. You're the one who's not learning science or social studies."

E.J. tried to say something, but Hannah waved her quiet. "You'll have to keep cheating all your life to cover up what you haven't learned. Then what kind of veterinarian will you be? The kind who doesn't know what she's doing. I wouldn't want to take my dog to a vet like that. And I don't think I want to be friends with a person like that either."

Then she turned and ran before E.J. could say a word.

Hannah went through the rest of the day without speaking to E.J. She went to lunch late and ate alone. When Ms. Cho gave them time to study for the next social studies test, she asked to go to the library. She rushed home after school and studied alone in her room.

A Friend's Business

The next morning, Ms. Cho announced, "It's time for our social studies test. Let's put our books away and get our pencils out."

Hannah felt a tap on her shoulder. "Nicholas, go away," she muttered. He tapped again. "Nicholas!" Hannah whirled around.

Nicholas was holding E.J.'s calculator/diary. "E.J. said to pass this to you," he reported.

Hannah looked at E.J., but she had her head turned away. Before she could send any message, Ms. Cho had dropped the test on her desk. Hannah forgot about E.J. while she struggled with longitude and latitude.

When she went up to put her test on Ms. Cho's desk,

A Friend's Business

Hannah saw that E.J. was still working. A few minutes later, when E.J. passed by to hand in her test, she dropped a note on Hannah's desk.

Hannah unfolded it and read the message. "T.A.L.F."

Thanks a lot, friend, Hannah figured with a smile. She took a clean sheet of paper and wrote a message back. All it took was two letters.

"N.P."

The Stack and Attack Pack

Before his eyes were even open, Matthew remembered. *It's my birthday! Finally, I'll get my Stack and Attack Pack computer game.* For weeks, Matthew had talked about the new computer game. "It's great," he had explained to his older sister, Amanda. "The Attack Rangers each have their own tanks, jeeps, and helicopters. But when they need to, they can stack up and make one giant fighting machine."

"I see," Amanda had said. She was already grown up and married, but she always knew just what to buy him for Christmas or his birthday.

Something like the Stack and Attack Pack. As he ate breakfast, Matthew pretended to play it like they did on the TV commercials. "Zoooom!" he said through a mouthful of cereal, as he pretended the helicopter swooped low over the table.

"Shhh-boom!" He fired the pretend tank at his bowl.

Being thankful

"Rat-a-tat-a-tat!" He pretended to fire the machine gun on his jeep and shoot holes in the cereal box.

Rowf! Matthew's dog, Ralph, joined in.

Matthew's mother looked at him. "If your breakfast is quite dead now, perhaps you can go ahead and eat it. We need to go to the grocery store to get stuff for the party. Remind me to get more dog food. Ralph ate the last of his this morning."

When his friends arrived that afternoon, the house looked like a balloon factory. There were balloons covering one wall, balloons hanging from the ceiling, and balloons for each person.

"The first game," Matthew's mom announced, "is a water-balloon-catching contest. But in this game, the person catching it has to wear a blindfold."

"Oh no!" Sandi shouted. "You have to catch the first one, Matthew."

Out on the backyard patio, Sandi grabbed a red balloon and tossed it up. "Are you ready, Matthew?"

"Not yet," Matthew mumbled through the blindfold. "How far away are you?"

"Just about ten steps," Sandi answered. "Now put your hands up."

"Come on, Matthew," Corey shouted. "Try catching it with your teeth!"

Sandi tossed the balloon right at Matthew's chest. *Bonk!* It bounced off without breaking. "Hey," Matthew shouted as his hands waved wildly, "what happened?"

The balloon didn't break when it hit the ground either. As it bounced and rolled away, Ralph rushed after it. *Rowf!* Then the dog's teeth snapped on it. *Pop-splat!*

Ralph tilted his head and sniffed. *Rowf?* He seemed to bark a question. The look on his face when he turned to look at Matthew made the shouting and laughing start all over.

Everyone enjoyed the cake and ice cream. Especially Ralph, who begged from one person to the next. Finally, it was time to open the presents.

"Thanks for the dinosaur eraser covers, Sandi," Matthew said when he opened the present she brought. "Thanks for the puzzle book," he said to Angelica. "Thanks, this is great!" he said to Corey when he pulled out the water-squirting base-ball. "This will drive Ralph crazy."

He got an excellent color-it-yourself poster and color marker set from his parents (and clothes, of course). The tag on the next present only said "To Matthew." But he recognized the writing. It had to be from Amanda. And it was just the right size for a Stack and Attack Pack game. He smiled at his sister as he ripped the paper off.

The Stack and Attack Pack

"It's a . . . model." It was a model of a jet fighter plane, the kind you have to put together. It wasn't the Stack and Attack Pack at all. Matthew looked at the box for a second, then set it down and picked up his squirting baseball.

"Matthew, did you forget to thank your sister?" his mother asked in her I-can't-believe-you're-acting-this-way voice.

"Oh, thanks," he said, hardly looking at Amanda. "Let's go try this baseball outside with Ralph," he called to Corey and the others.

That evening, his mom knocked and came in. "Matthew, I was a little disappointed in how you acted today," she said.

"I wanted a Stack and Attack Pack," Matthew said. "I never wanted to put together a model plane."

"Amanda wanted to give you something new—something you haven't tried before," Mom said. "Besides, you've never put together a model plane. You might like it."

"I know I would like a Stack and Attack Pack," Matthew muttered.

Mom looked over at the unopened model box on the shelf. "So you're not even going to touch it?" She shook her head. "It sure is hard to enjoy giving to someone who isn't thankful. Don't forget to feed your dog before you go to bed."

Ralph came in, looking at Matthew with sad eyes. "Don't look at me like that," Matthew said. Ralph jumped up on the bed. "I just wanted something else," Matthew said softly, more to himself than to the dog.

Rowf! Ralph barked.

"All right, you want your supper," Matthew said as he headed for the door. "Come on." The dog raced ahead. "I know you can hardly wait. You saw me carry in that new super-crunchy Dog Power food."

Matthew lifted the new bag out of the pantry and ripped it open. "Here, try this," he said, holding out a chunk. Ralph sniffed it, then wrinkled his nose and turned away.

"Hey, this stuff is supposed to be great," Matthew called after him. "The commercial says, 'Dogs will jump for joy when they eat it.' I want to see some jumping!"

He filled Ralph's bowl and called him back over. "Now, try it again. You'll like it."

Ralph took one sniff and jumped—away. He went back to his pillow.

"Well, of all the ungrateful dogs. I just wanted to give you something different—something I know you'd like if you just tried it. But no, you don't like it, so you're not even going to touch it. Fine. I hope you starve!"

Matthew stomped back to his room, still annoyed with Ralph. As he stepped in, he saw the model box on the shelf. Suddenly, the things he had said to Ralph sounded very familiar.

Oops, he thought. He picked up the model plane box and looked at the picture. *It does look neat,* he thought. *I wonder how hard it is to put together?*

In a few minutes, he had all the pieces laid out on his desk. He looked at the instruction sheet. *This must be part of a wing, and this is the landing gear.* Matthew worked on the model for a few minutes and then snapped two pieces together.

"Hey," he said out loud, "this is fun. It's like a puzzle." He looked back into the box. "And when it's done, I get to paint it and decorate it with these stickers." When he picked up the sheet of stickers, another paper fell out.

He recognized the writing. "When your model plane is

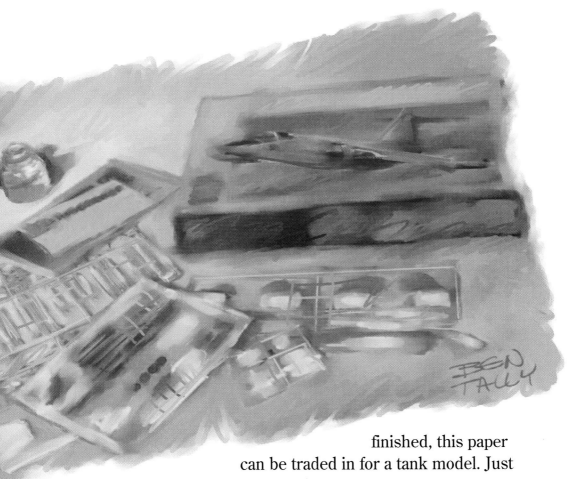

finished, this paper can be traded in for a tank model. Just bring it to me! Love, Amanda."

Matthew went to the phone and dialed her number. "Hi, Amanda, it's me. The model jet is great! . . . Yeah, that's what I want to do. And then I can show it to the guys at school. . . . If I need help, will you come over?"

Matthew listened for a minute. Then he said, "Amanda, I'm sorry about how I acted. I should have known you'd get me something great."

Then next morning, he noticed that Ralph's bowl was empty. "I knew you'd like that stuff," he said. "Aren't you glad I bought it for you?"

Rowf!

MRS. MCCUSKY'S CAT

Come on, Janelle. I'll show you a shortcut." Lisa led her new friend through the narrow alley between two buildings.

"Does this take us to Seventh Street?" Janelle asked. "Isn't that the street beside our apartments?"

"Shhh!" Lisa hissed. "You have to be quiet. Now, stoop down," she went on in a whisper. "We have to be very quiet so we won't wake up Lucifer."

"Lucifer?" Janelle froze. "Who's that?"

"Keep down!" Lisa looked anxiously toward the fence beside them. "Hurry!"

Janelle's next step sent a can clattering across the pavement. From behind the fence came the sound of running feet.

"Run!" Lisa shouted.

Bawr-awr-awrk! The sound exploded by Janelle's head as Lucifer leap against the fence beside her. She didn't bother to scream—she just ran.

Living in a bad neighborhood; dealing with drugs

"Keep going," Lisa huffed as she grabbed Janelle's arm and hurried her out onto Seventh Street.

"What's the hurry?" Janelle asked, breathing hard. "We're past the dog."

"Lucifer's not the dangerous one. Every time he barks, Mr. Thompson comes out shouting about burglars and waving a gun. Come on, this way."

Janelle stopped. "But isn't that our apartment building down there?" she asked, pointing east on Seventh Street.

"Yes," Lisa answered, "but we're going to cross over on Lincoln Avenue and walk up Eighth Street."

"Why?"

Lisa grabbed Janelle's arm and pointed. "See that green car? That's Anthony's car. When he's hanging around down at that corner, we go the other way."

Janelle stared. "That's a great car. What's the problem?"

"He buys and sells drugs," Lisa said plainly. "And Mr. Thompson thinks Anthony's the one who's been robbing people's apartments. Anyway, when he's out there, we go around the long way and walk back up Paine Street. Then we can go in through the back door."

Lisa could see that Janelle wasn't sure. "Janelle, I don't know what your old neighborhood was like, but things are different here. Just do what I say, please? Come on, I'll take you by Mrs. McCusky's."

"Where?"

Lisa laughed. "Mrs. McCusky is a friend of my mom's. And a friend of mine. She lives in this building." Lisa guided her friend up the steps. "Mom lets me stop here on the way home if I want to. And I always want to. Mrs. McCusky makes the best oatmeal cookies in the world."

A knock at Apartment 120 brought a small silver-haired woman to the door. "Why, hello, Lisa. How are you this fine day? Let me unhook this chain so you can come on in."

Lisa said, "This is Janelle. Her family moved into our building this week. We were just on our way home after school. I told her I knew where to find the best cookies in the world."

"Well, you ought to know—you've been here often enough. Welcome, Janelle. You'll find that my house has cookies most every day. I find it a pleasure to have youngsters about."

While she spoke, a large gray cat rubbed against her leg. Purr, purr. Janelle knelt down beside it. "What's your cat's name?"

Mrs. McCusky frowned, but a smile was hiding in her eyes. "That's Rigby. He's a pest. Always leaving hair everywhere, meowing and purring. I don't know why I keep him."

Rigby met Janelle's petting with more purrs. "He's a nice cat," Janelle said. "I think he likes me."

Mrs. McCusky snorted. "He likes anyone who will take the time to pet him. Or feed him. Lisa, would you open a can of cat food while you're here? You know how much trouble I have with that can opener."

"Sure, Mrs. McCusky," Lisa said. She reached into the cupboard and pulled out a can. The sound of the phone interrupted her. *Ring!*

"Oh, Janelle, you have to see this. Watch Rigby." They both stared as Rigby ran from Janelle's feet to the phone.

Ring!

"Meow," Rigby said as he jumped up on the table beside the phone. "Meow?"

Ring!

"What is he doing?" Janelle asked. Rigby answered the question himself. He batted at the phone. "Meow," he said again.

"He's trying to answer it!" Janelle gasped. "What a smart cat!"

"What a pain," Mrs. McCusky grumbled. "Out of the way, Rigby. Hello? Oh, it's you, Eleanor."

Janelle turned to Lisa. "Does Rigby always do that?"

Lisa nodded. "Sometimes he even knocks the receiver off and meows into it." She finished opening the can and dumped the food into the cat's bowl. "Here, Rigby. Come and eat."

The girls ate their cookies as Mrs. McCusky talked. Just as they were ready to slip out the door, Mrs. McCusky said goodbye and hung up. "Sorry about that, girls. My friend Eleanor calls most every afternoon to talk."

"That's OK," Lisa said. "We need to get home anyway. Thanks for the cookies. See you later."

As they walked out onto the street, Lisa looked back down the street. "Anthony's still there. Let's go." Janelle took a long look at the green car, then turned and followed her friend.

The next afternoon, the school door slammed behind Lisa. *Great,* she thought as she hurried toward home, *I have play practice on the night before our math test.*

On her way down Seventh Street, Lisa was too busy thinking over her part in the play to notice the green car. She didn't

notice until she heard laughing voices from up ahead.

Before she could turn and go the other way, Lisa recognized one of the voices. "Janelle?" she whispered. There was her friend, leaning against the green hood, wearing a nervous smile.

Anthony, in his dark shades, stood right beside her.

Janelle, get away from him, Lisa shouted to herself. She stood where she was, too afraid of Anthony to get any closer. As she watched, Anthony reached into his pocket and pulled out a plastic bag.

Without another thought, Lisa ran toward the green car. "Janelle! Janelle, come here. I have to tell you something! Hurry!"

Janelle laughed nervously. "Lisa, I'm talking to Anthony. You come over here."

"No!" Lisa shouted. "Janelle, come on."

Janelle shrugged at Anthony and took two steps toward her friend. "Lisa, I'm just being friendly. Anthony seems nice. It's OK."

Lisa grabbed Janelle's arm. "It's not OK," she hissed. "Anthony isn't nice. He's just being friendly because he wants to give you drugs. Come on, let's go!" She pulled, but Janelle balked.

"I'm not going to take any drugs," she insisted. "It won't hurt to talk for a minute."

"Yeah, baby," a rough voice purred in Lisa's ear. It was Anthony. "It won't hurt at all. We can all be friends—there's enough for everyone." The gold rings on his fingers flashed as he opened his hand to show the plastic bag of red pills. "Wanna try some fun?"

SAY "NO!"

N o!" Lisa shouted. "And leave my friend alone, or I'll call the police!" She yanked Janelle toward the building.

But Anthony's voice followed them. "Better mind your own business, girl. This can be a dangerous place to live."

"I wasn't going to take any," Janelle protested once the door closed behind them. "I was just talking to him."

Lisa put her hand over her pounding heart as they both collapsed onto the stairway. "That's what my brother said. He was just hanging around, being one of the guys. But they kept after him to just 'Try it.' Finally, he did."

"So?" Janelle shrugged.

Lisa jumped to her feet. "I only get to see him once a month now, because he's in the state prison. He told me that the only way to handle drugs and drug dealers is to just say 'no!' Say it fast, and get away."

**Living in a bad neighborhood;
dealing with drugs**

Janelle's eyes got big, but she didn't say anything else. "Come on," Lisa finally said, "let's go study for our math test. Mom will be home soon—maybe she'll take us to the park."

The next afternoon, Janelle chattered about gym class all the way home. But Lisa was careful to watch for the green car. Since only a white car sat in front of their building, she led the way toward Seventh Street.

"Ms. Wilson said I should try out for basketball," Janelle said as she walked along, just behind Lisa. "I can shoot better than most of the girls on the B-team already . . . Whoa! What did you stop for?"

Lisa had frozen on the sidewalk. She stared at the red-

and-blue lights on top of the white car in front of their building. Janelle stared too. "The police—Lisa, you didn't call them, did you?"

Lisa shook her head. "No. Maybe it's something else.

Maybe it doesn't have anything to do with Anthony."

"I hope not," Janelle said. She glanced around. "Oh no. Don't look behind you!"

"Why not?" Lisa whispered as her neck swiveled. The sight of Anthony's green car cruising slowly behind them made her turn back even faster. "Where did he come from? Did he see us?"

"Of course he saw us," Janelle hissed back. "He could almost spit on us from there. Shouldn't we just turn around and be friendly? You know, just talk to him?"

The look on Lisa's face answered that question. "Come on," she said. "Let's go around the long way." They ran without looking back. "Now we'll just go in the back way," Lisa said between breaths.

"Look!" Janelle stopped breathing and pointed. A green car turned the corner. It was Anthony.

Lisa grabbed her friend's arm and turned around. "We have to get off the street. He must have been wondering if I called the police. But since we ran to get away from him, he's probably sure I did." She turned toward the closest apartment building.

Almost without thinking, Lisa headed for Mrs. McCusky's apartment. She whispered as she knocked, "Let's not say anything about you-know-who."

"Who is it?" a tiny voice from inside asked.

"It's just Lisa and Janelle," Lisa called. The knob turned, and the door opened as far as the chain would let it.

"I should have known it would be you," Mrs. McCusky said with a laugh as she pushed the door closed enough to unhook the chain. "You must have followed the smell of cookies coming out of the oven."

The girls relaxed with the warm cookies while Mrs. McCusky talked about her day. "I've been having trouble with the sink in the bathroom for weeks. First, it was just a drip. Drip, drip, drip. But now, it's running all the time. Finally, the manager stopped to see about it. He's says he's sending a

plumber this afternoon."

As she spoke, there was a knock at the apartment door. "That's probably him now," Mrs. McCusky said, shuffling toward the sound. She hooked the chain and turned the knob, slipping the door open. "Are you the plumber?" she asked.

Crack! Lisa set down her glass of milk just as the door smashed in, pulling the chain halfway out of the wall.

"No!" Mrs. McCusky shouted. "Stay out!" She pushed against the door, but it didn't help.

Crash! The door crashed in so hard it knocked over the hat rack behind it. Janelle screamed as Mrs. McCusky stumbled back and tripped over the footstool. She fell against the couch with a terrifying thud.

"Mrs. McCusky!" Lisa shouted as she jumped up. She pushed past Janelle and ran toward the fallen woman.

"Just hold it right there," a low, threatening voice said. Both girls froze when they saw a short man wearing a ski mask standing in the doorway. In his hand was a long silver knife.

Lisa stared at the knife. She had to bite her lip to keep her teeth from chattering, but she said, "Mrs. McCusky's hurt. I have to help her."

"Get back in the kitchen," the man commanded. He closed the door as he waved her back with his knife. "I'll see about the old woman."

Lisa backed up and fell into a chair. Janelle was still sitting, frozen, except for the tears running down her face.

"I don't see no blood," the rough voice behind the mask said. "The old woman's just knocked out."

"What do you want?" Janelle squeaked out.

The eyes in the mask glanced around. "I been meaning to

check out this place for a long time. You never know what kind of treasures old people keep. But what am I going to do with the two of you?"

Just the sound of his voice sent shivers down the goosebumps on Lisa's skin. Janelle clamped her eyes shut and started a chant. "Oh no. Oh no. Oh no. Oh no . . ."

HELP IN A FUR COAT

T he first thing you're gonna do is shut up," the masked man growled. He grabbed a dish towel off the counter and stuffed one end of it in Janelle's mouth. Janelle's eyes never opened.

"I got a message to both of you from Anthony," he said as he snatched the extension cord off the kitchen fan. "He says you better keep out of his business. And keep your mouth shut." He sliced the cord in half and knelt down to tie Janelle's hands behind the chair.

Lisa's breath was coming in short little huffs. She had never been so scared. *What am I going to do?* she thought. She glanced over at Mrs. McCusky's still form by the couch. *I hope she's OK.* She grunted as her hands were yanked behind the chair and tied. *I hope I'm OK!*

The robber yanked the towel out from under the cooling cookies and shoved it in Lisa's mouth. Then he disappeared down the hall toward the bedroom.

> **Living in a bad neighborhood;
> dealing with drugs**

By now, Lisa was starting to see sparkles in the air. *Calm down,* she told herself. *Take a deep breath.* She couldn't breathe around the towel, so she inhaled through her nose. *It's a good thing I don't have a cold.* She started feeling better. *At least this towel smells good.*

Lisa looked over at Janelle. Her eyes were open, and she was looking around wildly. "Mmm me mome?" she tried to ask through the towel.

Lisa shook her head and tilted it toward the bedroom. Just then, the robber reappeared, stuffing something into his pocket.

He pointed a long finger at them. "Someone will find you before long. But when they do, you're not gonna remember anything about me. Got it?"

Both girls nodded, but Lisa was staring at the robber's hand. Her eyes got big when she recognized the gold rings on his fingers.

As soon as the door closed behind him, Lisa began trying to spit out the towel. She couldn't. She pulled on the cords that tied her hands, but they didn't give at all.

Janelle spit her towel out quickly. "Aaack! Lisa, I'm so scared."

"Mmmm! Mm Mm!" Lisa tried to speak.

Janelle got the message. "Scoot over close to me," she said. Lisa scooted and leaned. Janelle grabbed the end of Lisa's towel with her teeth and yanked it out.

"Quiet, Janelle. He might still be nearby," Lisa said as soon as she could talk. She looked over at the floor by the couch. "Mrs. McCusky, are you OK? Can you hear me, Mrs. McCusky?" Now Lisa's voice was filled with tears. "Please hear me!"

The two girls looked at each other and agreed without saying a word. "Help!" they both screamed. "Help, we're tied up! Mrs. McCusky's hurt! Help us, please!"

A few minutes later, the silence brought no answers. "Everyone must be gone," Janelle finally said.

"Or too afraid to help," Lisa agreed. "What are we going to do? Mrs. McCusky might be really hurt." The quiet of the apartment was the only answer.

Finally, Janelle spoke. "You don't think Anthony's coming back, do you?"

Lisa was surprised. "You figured out that it was Anthony?"

Janelle nodded. "I thought I knew his voice. Then I saw the gold rings. He followed us here." She nodded at Mrs. McCusky. "All this is my fault. I should have listened to you."

Lisa shook her head. "It's not your fault he's a bad person. At least you know he's bad for sure now." While she was speaking, they heard a sound from the back room.

"Oh no! Is he back?" Janelle closed her eyes again, and Lisa held her breath.

"Meow?"

"Rigby, you scared us to death!" Lisa let out her breath. "I don't suppose you'd come over here and chew on this cord to show how sorry you are."

All Rigby wanted was a scratch behind the ears. When no one in the kitchen would scratch, he went to his owner. "Meow?" he called, rubbing against her hand.

"That's it, Rigby," Lisa said. "Wake her up. Wake up, Mrs. McCusky!" But there was no response.

"Is she going to die?" Janelle whispered.

Before Lisa could answer, another sound split the air. *Ring!* Rigby ran to the phone.

Ring!

"Meow," Rigby said as he jumped up beside the phone. "Mer-reow?"

Suddenly, Lisa felt a little hope. "Come on, Rigby, answer it!"

Ring!

"Meow?"

"Come on, Rigby!"

Janelle looked at Lisa. "What's wrong with you? He can't answer it."

Ring!

Lisa turned to Janelle. "He can knock the receiver off. And

that's probably Mrs. McCusky's friend Eleanor. If Rigby
knocks it off, we can shout for help. Eleanor might hear us."

"Meow?" Rigby batted at the phone.

"Come on, Rigby, you can do it!" both girls urged.

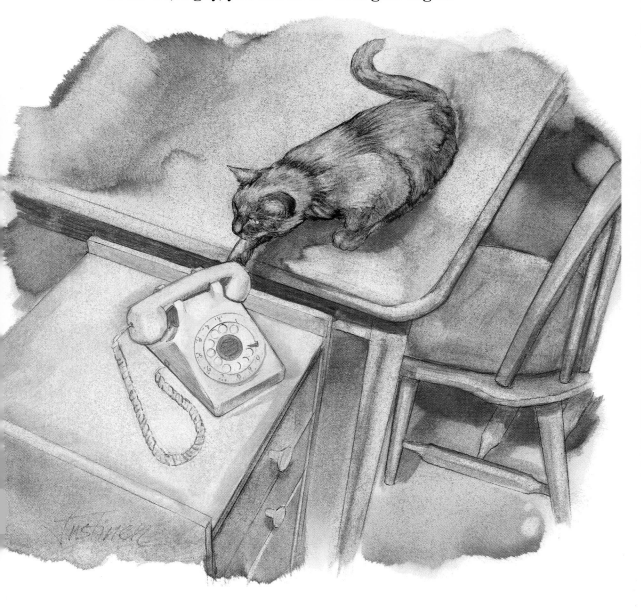

Ring! Rigby batted again, and this time the receiver fell to the floor.

"Help!" Lisa shouted. "Call the police! Mrs. McCusky is hurt! Call 911!"

Just then, they heard a voice from the hallway. "Lisa, is that you? Are you OK?"

For a second, Lisa thought she was dreaming. Then she snapped out of it. "Mom! We're at Mrs. McCusky's! Help!"

The broken door blasted open. "Lisa!" Mom ran to her side.

"I'm OK," Lisa cried. "But Mrs. McCusky's hurt. Help her, please." Mom took one look and grabbed the phone off the floor.

"What? Oh, Eleanor, it's you. I don't know. Can you call 911? Good. I'll stay with her here." Mom put down the phone and untied the girls. Lisa threw her arms around her mother's neck. Finally, everything was going to be OK.

On the way home from school a few weeks later, Janelle was complaining about basketball practice. "Coach even made us run laps today."

Lisa laughed. "Play practice is a lot easier." They turned down Eighth Street like they did every day now. This time, the door to Apartment 120 was standing open.

Lisa felt a shiver go down her backbone. "Mrs. McCusky? Are you there?"

"Right in here, girls," Mrs. McCusky called from the kitchen. "The plumber's been going in and out all afternoon, so I just left the door open. Like I was telling Mr. Thompson this morning, it feels a bit safer around here with that Anthony in jail. You girls did this neighborhood a big favor by reporting him to the police."

Janelle smiled at Lisa. "We're just glad you're OK, Mrs.

McCusky. We need your cookies."

"Meow?" Rigby walked in, crying for attention.

Lisa laughed and bent down to scratch his ears. "You're right, Rigby. You were the real hero."

Rigby just purred.